"*Half in Love* is an original mix of quiet calm and wrenching pain. Meloy's gracefully confident, subtly emotional voice brings her locales vividly to life."

—Susan Adams, *Washington Post*

"Memorable . . . In an era when story writers seem to be compelled to link their stories thematically into one tight package, *Half in Love* shows that sometimes alternating the flavor can improve the whole. . . . Like Pam Houston and Judy Blunt, Meloy has a uniquely female perspective on what life in the West is like for women. . . . She's left a crisp, indelible picture of a place most readers will never have the privilege of visiting. With this promising debut she allows readers to live there for a little while."

—John Freeman, *San Francisco Chronicle*

"Throughout these bite-size stories, Maile Meloy has a flair for making uncertainty vivid, for providing oblique answers in the form of startling enigmas, and for making the improbable seem palpably real. . . . Meloy's voice is as unvarnished as her characters and as unadorned as a Montana hillside."

—Mark Rozzo, *Los Angeles Times*

"Meloy writes with keen insight and compassion."

—Sybil Downing, *The Denver Post*

"Meloy's assured prose probes the minds of Montana ranch girls with astounding aplomb."

—Gillian Flynn, *Entertainment Weekly*

"With her deceptively unfancy writing, Meloy excels at moments that make readers feel slightly sick with grief. Though her stories are sad, they're not sentimental. She can even be quite funny, usually through her astute observations of character."

—Polly Shulman, *Newsday*

"Beautifully written."

—*Harper's Bazaar*

"Glowing high-plains tales . . . The seduction is immediate."

—Lisa Shea, *Elle*

"Maile Meloy writes with both fearlessness and true compassion, two talents that are rarely combined. In every story she creates a complex portrait of such disparate lives that by the end of the book I feel like I've seen the world. *Half in Love* is a vibrant, gorgeous collection."

—Ann Patchett, author of
The Magician's Assistant and *Bel Canto*

"The stories' fit and polish are remarkable, they are right on the dime with cadence and timing. And Meloy is fearless in the sweep of her attentions, commanding the manners, idioms, and fundaments of a range of cultures, regions, and classes. Trust this audacious writer. She is a wonder."

—Geoffrey Wolff, author of
The Duke of Deception and *The Age of Consent*

"Maile Meloy's stories will make writers jealous and readers jubilant. Her knack for characters and situations as diverse as they are genuine is uncanny, unerring, and hugely exciting."

—Myla Goldberg, author of *Bee Season*

"Maile Meloy is a true and rare find—a natural who consistently widens and extends the short story form to meet the demands of her uncommon intelligence and wit and sympathy. She possesses grace and subtlety, and with this first suite of stories, seems in fact to have arrived fully formed."

—Richard Ford, author of
Independence Day and *Rock Springs*

HALF IN LOVE

✦ STORIES ✦

MAILE MELOY

SCRIBNER

New York London Toronto Sydney Singapore

For Nick Halpern

SCRIBNER
1230 Avenue of the Americas
New York, NY 10020

First Scribner trade paperback edition 2003

SCRIBNER and design are trademarks of
Macmillan Library Reference USA, Inc., used under license
by Simon & Schuster, the publisher of this work.

For information about special discounts for bulk purchases,
please contact Simon & Schuster Special Sales:
1-800-456-6798 or business@simonandschuster.com

Designed by Kyoko Watanabe
Text set in Berthold Garamond

Manufactured in the United States of America

3   5   7   9   10   8   6   4   2

The Library of Congress has cataloged the Scribner edition as follows:
Meloy, Maile.
Half in love : stories / by Maile Meloy.
p. cm.
1. West (U.S.)—Social life and customs—Fiction.
2. Women—West (U.S.)—Fiction. I. Title.
PS3613.E46 H35 2002
813'.6—dc21
2001054217

ISBN 0-7432-1647-4
0-7432-4685-3 (Pbk)

Some of these stories have been published in slightly different form:
"Ranch Girl" *(The New Yorker)*, "Aqua Boulevard" *(The Paris Review)*, "Tome"
(Best American Voices 2000), "The River" and "The Ice Harvester" *(Faultline)*, "Kite
Whistler Aquamarine" *(Witness)*, "Native Sandstone" *(Ploughshares)*, "Four Lean
Hounds, ca. 1976" *(The Ontario Review)*

CONTENTS

HALF IN LOVE

TOME

FOR EIGHT MONTHS, I had been telling my client he had no tort claim. Sawyer had worked construction for thirty years, building houses for people with Montana fantasies. He was putting up a roof when one of the trusses fell, collapsing the others and taking him down with them. He started to have fainting spells and memory loss and couldn't work. We got a settlement, not a great one but not bad. The contractor was clearly negligent, having failed to brace the trusses, but workers' compensation precluded the tort claim—we couldn't sue.

Sawyer had worked active, outside jobs all his life, and suddenly he could do nothing. It seemed to be the idleness, more than the brain damage, that made him crazy. He couldn't read, because the words came out scrambled, and he could barely sit still to try. He phoned me three times a day. My secretary stopped putting his calls through, so he came to the office, on foot because they wouldn't let him drive. He was a big, graying, blond-bearded man, my father's age, muscular but getting fat without his work. He treated me like a daughter, scolding and cajoling me. He wanted to sue, demanded to sue. His wife was sick of his moping at the house, and his friends had been the men he'd worked with; he'd lost everything he liked about his life. I knew workers' comp and I tried to explain: he'd gotten what he was going to get. There was nothing more I could do for him.

Finally I found a tort lawyer in Billings, four hours east, who was willing to give him another opinion. I had to be in Bozeman anyway, halfway there, so I drove over and met Sawyer and his wife at the lawyer's office. I didn't think Sawyer, frustrated and hair-triggered as he was, should be making his case alone, with his wife jumping in and correcting him. The lawyer was a thin man in a dark suit and a big leather chair. There were antelope heads on the walls, bear claws as book-ends. We explained the situation. The lawyer said, "You have no tort claim."

Sawyer said, "Okay."

I thought, *That's* what it's like to be a man. If I were a man I could explain the law and people would listen and say, "Okay." It would be so restful.

We went back outside. The lawyer's office had a view of the cliffs. We'd been in Billings fifteen minutes and had nothing to do but drive home. My client shook my hand, and his wife, a small, curly-haired woman who had been pretty once, gave me a quick motherly hug. She smelled like roses and cigarettes. When I stopped at the mall for a sandwich, they pulled up in the parking space next to mine. Sawyer got out of the car screaming at his wife about her fucking attitude, grabbed his jacket from the seat and slammed the door.

He said, "I'm going in your car." His wife peeled out of the lot and turned toward the highway.

We stood alone in the parking lot, my client and I, and then I told him I wasn't going yet, and he climbed in my passenger seat to wait. His head touched the ceiling of my car. I offered to get him lunch and he shook his head like a great, sulky child. So I left him there and walked the length of the mall twice, eating my sandwich. When I returned, he hadn't moved: jacket in his lap, eyes on his knees, he waited for his ride.

Before we were out of Billings he said the only thing to do was get a machine gun and kill everyone. I stopped the car. I said I wouldn't have him talking like that, and told him to get out. No one knew where I was, and Sawyer weighed twice what I did, but I wasn't afraid, I was only tired of him. He promised not to do it again.

At the first sign for the turnoff to Red Lodge, outside Laurel, Sawyer said, "I wish my wife would roll over on the highway."

I stopped the car on the shoulder and said, "I swear, I'll leave you in Laurel."

Twenty miles on he began a low, keening rant about his negligent boss, about his negligent wife, about how no one understood how miserable he was. I told him if he opened his mouth for the rest of the drive I would let him out wherever we were. He didn't bridle. He didn't say anything at all. I found a country station to fill the silence, and Sawyer began to weep. He sobbed in the passenger seat all the way home, without saying a word.

*

A week later my phone rang in the middle of the night. I was sleeping alone then, and there was nothing to do but answer it. A call in the night could mean anything. This one meant Sawyer had a hostage and a gun at the state fund building and wanted me to look at his workers' comp file. The hostage specialists in town, such as they were, said I didn't have to go in. But I was afraid of what they might do to him, so I stood in front of my closet deciding whether to wear lawyer clothes or not, then pulled on jeans and put a bra on under the sweatshirt I'd slept in. In the parking lot behind the building, the cops had three patrol cars, the bureau chief from the office, and a big thermos of coffee. They had Sawyer on the telephone, and said he was calm. The hostage was a night watchman, a Samoan kid who'd come here to play football at the college. I'd known his name once, something long with *a*'s and *n*'s in it, but everyone called him Big Man. I was impressed, just for a moment, that my client had taken Big Man down.

I drank the coffee while the bureau chief drew me a map of the office. They gave me keys and a heavy, bulletproof vest, and I changed awkwardly in the back of a squad car, the vest cold under my sweatshirt, against my skin. The officer who helped me fasten it had written a report for a child-support case of mine, including the line, "The defendant instructed me to consume feces." I'd always liked him. He socked me on the shoulder and told me to do good, and I went in.

The building was four stories, dark brick, at the end of the old gold-rush main street. It was dark inside, and the bottom floor was all cubicles, the burlap-faced dividers hung with calendars and cartoons. I found my way to the stairs by the light of screen savers and exit signs, and walked up to the third floor, where my client was keeping Big Man.

"Sawyer?" I called, as I came out of the stairwell into another dark maze of cubicles. "It's me. I'm here to find your file."

I heard a rustling noise, but no one answered.

"Should I come to you or go get the file?" I asked.

Sawyer's voice came out of the gloom, hoarse and tired. "Go get the file," he said.

I couldn't tell which cubicle the voice came from, but it was on the east side of the building, to my right. The cops had told me to engage in conversation. "Is Big Man okay?" I asked.

"His name is Amituana," Sawyer said. "Did you know he's a member of the Samoan royal family?"

"I didn't," I said. I followed the bureau chief's map to the big beige file cabinet where they kept the dead files. The lock on the cabinet had a tiny six on it, and I flipped through the ring of keys until I found the six. I asked, "Does that make him a prince?"

Two low voices conferred. Then came a voice an octave lower than Sawyer's. "Sort of," Big Man said. "If fourteen people die, I will be king."

I found Sawyer's file, a fat brown accordion, under *S*. "How likely is that?" I asked.

There was another pause. "Not very," Big Man's voice said.

I could see the room well now, by the exit signs and the streetlights. "I have the file," I called. "What should I do?"

"We're in the third cubicle from the door," Sawyer said. "Near the windows. With the horse calendar."

Big Man sat cross-legged on the floor, hands tied behind his back with orange baling twine, and Sawyer sat in one of those kneeling chairs that support the lower back, by a computer screen with changing photographs of the sea. He rested a hunting rifle on his knee, and seemed to have hung up the phone on the police. The two men filled the entire space. Big Man had close-cropped hair and a narrow mustache with a goatee.

"We've been talking football," Sawyer said.

Big Man said, "He played both offense and defense in college." He seemed genuinely impressed.

"It was a junior college," Sawyer explained. He looked at me in my sweatshirt, bulked by the Kevlar vest underneath. "Sorry to get you out of bed," he said. "Sit down."

I sat in the remaining floor space next to Big Man, who nodded. He was carrying himself beautifully, no dishonor to his family or his future subjects.

"Read me the file," Sawyer said. "Not the stuff I said, just the stuff they said about me. I want to hear all the letters."

"That'll take all night," I said.

"So start."

I began to read in the dim light. One of the computer's ocean scenes was darker than the others, and each time the dark one came around the reading was harder. I read the letters from the insurance adjuster to the bureau chief, the memos from the chief's secretary to her boss, the letters from Sawyer's employer's attorney. I read letters by me, dictated too quickly, sounding too lawyerly, typed up by my secretary and flung into the afternoon mail. What wasn't embarrassing was sad, and what wasn't sad was stultifying, but Sawyer sat riveted. I looked up from time to time to see if I could stop. He gestured me on with the rifle in his hand. I read through the neurologist's account of what Sawyer could do, and through the settlement. I read the figure Sawyer was to receive for the loss of his work.

"You got screwed," Big Man said.

"Thank you," Sawyer said, with no irony in his voice, only relief that someone else could see the injustice. "What can I do now?" he asked me. "Tell me, now, what can I do?"

"Give yourself up."

"No, I'm serious here. I mean about the claim."

I looked at the heavy stack of papers in my lap. "I don't think you can do anything," I said. "Go to physical therapy, be nice to your wife."

"She's gone," he said. "No, that's all over. This is over, too, isn't it? It's a wrapped-up case."

I nodded. It was in with the dead files. And finality was the effect of the letters, read together: it was a thing done.

"I'm letting Amituana go," Sawyer said. He helped the kid to his feet, which was a struggle with the rifle in one hand, the kid's wrists tied and both men so heavy. Amituana staggered back against a cubicle divider and it shuddered, and then they were both upright. "He's got a country to rule," Sawyer said. "Fourteen people could die, easy."

He brushed off the kid's clothes with his free hand. "If you get to be king of Samoa and I show up there," he said, "you'll have a job for me, right? You'll remember I got screwed and I let you go?"

"Sure," Big Man said.

"Okay," Sawyer said. "You take the stairs and go outside, and tell them if they try anything I'll kill the woman. She's my lawyer, I've got reason to kill her. Tell them that."

I looked at Sawyer to see if he was serious, but I couldn't tell.

"Okay," Big Man said.

Sawyer turned him around and clapped him on one of his great halfback shoulders, and the kid nodded at both of us like he was leaving a party. He walked off toward the staircase, trailing orange twine from his bound wrists.

"He's a good kid," Sawyer said as we watched him go. The heavy, careful steps died away on the stairs below. Then Sawyer turned to me.

"You can still help me," he said.

"If you turn yourself in," I said, "we can gin up a mental distress defense, get you a good lawyer for it."

"Nope," Sawyer said. He checked his watch. "I'll slip out the front, where they don't expect me. You go out the back, to the parking lot where you came in, and keep them busy. Stand in the door and pretend I've got the gun on you, and relay messages to the cops like I'm hiding there. Say I want a car, and I want three thousand dollars, and I want an hour's head start. Okay? Afterward, they'll never know I wasn't there with the gun. Just give me a chance to get out the front and get away."

He was calm and seemed sane, even with the rifle in his hand. He was just my client, still in a bad spot, still wanting me to help him, and I was trying.

"Aren't there cops out front?"

"I've been watching," he said. "They've all stayed out back, where I told them I'd come out. So will you do it?"

I said okay. There was no arguing with him, and nothing else I could say. He called 911 and we waited while the operator figured out how to patch him through to the squad cars below. I asked him again to give up and he said no. He told them we were coming out. We went downstairs with both my wrists held behind me, his grip warm and damp but not tight. Then he took the office keys and told me to wait a minute before I went out. Crouched down, he dodged through the cubicle dividers to the front door. I heard a dead bolt scrape. Blue streetlight outlined his body, and he waved to me to go.

The back door was a fire door that opened without a key, and I pressed the bar and put a hand out to wave so they wouldn't shoot me, and then I stood with one hand behind my back, the door barely cracked. I thought I was going to do it, to play the part Sawyer had scripted for me, and then somehow it seemed impossible, a thing that was plausible back in the dark but now was not. He was a man with a gun. I stepped out with my hands up and said, "He's in front," but my voice cracked and I had to say it again, louder. "He's in front."

Sawyer wrote me a letter from prison. He said,

> It would sure be great if you came by. Tuesdays from 2–4 I can have visitors and it would be really something to see you. Or if you wrote a letter. You wouldn't believe how great it is to get a letter from the real world. On good days I can read okay now, and I can write back, and on bad days someone will read it to me. No one writes to me except my defense lawyer, and he's an asshole, and hardly writes anymore anyway. (Don't tell him I said he was an asshole. I know all you lawyers are tight.) And don't feel too bad about what happened. Of course they were out front. You did what you could do.

I kept the letter on top of my in-box for weeks, always moving it to the top, keeping it where I could see it, but I didn't write back. Whatever I could say to him would be so inadequate I couldn't imagine it on paper. I settled one case, started another, and the rest plodded along, piling up on my desk, while Sawyer's note kept floating to the top.

Finally, one cold blue Tuesday when the roads were dry, I left everything in the mess it was in, called a warden I knew for permission to bring food and picked up burgers on the way out to Deer Lodge. They brought Sawyer into the prison's visiting area and let us sit at the same table, no barrier at all. He'd lost the weight of the idle months, but he didn't look healthy. He looked pale, a little gray in the face, and older. We looked at each other awkwardly, like neither of us knew what we were doing there. The paper bags, still warm and smelling of fried things, felt heavy and wrong in my hands.

"I guess you've just had lunch," I said.

Sawyer gave me an appraising look. "Is there a shake in there?"

Sometimes I have a little luck—I had a chocolate shake and a vanilla one, still mostly frozen. We unpacked the bags and sat at the table, and Sawyer ate and talked about the inmates, using first names, telling stories that sounded like he'd planned them in his mind for someone to come from the outside and listen. He washed down burger with chocolate shake, sucked noisily through the straw.

"You know my wife's gone," he said finally. "You know where she went?"

I shook my head.

"When I stopped working and started getting crazy, she got a pen pal. A guy in prison in Wyoming. They wrote back and forth all year and I never knew. Then he got furloughed and she went to live with him. She sent me a letter that says they're living on a farm and have forty cats and she's never been so happy. Can you believe that? She mailed the letter from another town so I couldn't find her."

"Would you want to find her?"

"Yeah!" he said. "—No. I don't know. A guy in prison. I can't believe she found a guy in prison. I'm a guy in prison. What's wrong with me? But she would have left anyway."

"What did the guy do?"

"She won't tell me. Probably an ax murderer. It's Wyoming." He grinned and his face stretched into wrinkles he didn't have before, but the grin was charming. Sawyer was still game.

"So, you never wrote to me," he said, picking at the last of his fries. The bags and boxes and cups were strewn between us, empty now, an embarrassment of grease.

"I meant to," I said. "I kept meaning to."

"It wouldn't be so hard," he said. "You know?"

"I know."

"Man, you wouldn't believe how good mail feels. I think I told you that."

"I will, I'll write," I said. "I didn't know what to say."

"That's the thing, is you don't have to say anything special," he said. "I told you it's okay, about what happened. They would have got me anyway. I fucked up. But I mean this, you could talk about anything, talk about the weather, talk about your day. Just so you put it in an envelope and put it in the mail."

"Okay," I said.

"It doesn't have to be a tome," he said.

I drove home as the sky was beginning to darken. A sign in Deer Lodge advertised dinner theater, the Old Prison Players doing *Arsenic and Old Lace* at eight in the old stone prison building. I wondered where they found customers, but I didn't wonder enough to go be one.

I wasn't sleeping alone then, which was the only news in my life since I had seen Sawyer last, but I might as well have been. The guy was a prosecutor who never left the office before midnight, and sometimes then he'd stop by. So the evening stretched before me: long blue-gray clouds on the horizon, the abandoned work on my desk, my empty house. I could go back to the office, maybe catch my secretary locking up, say good night and stay to work until I was hungry again, and could get a bite to eat and a bath and go to bed. I would maybe be awakened to news of my prosecutor's militia case, and to sex, and then go back to sleep with another body in the bed.

It was a tolerable plan but I couldn't focus on it. What I did was watch the sky. As it changed, as the clouds stretched out and the orange flared up and pink reached out to meet the blue, I started thinking of it as a description, a letter, not a lawyer-sounding one, and not a tome, but a start, an account for Sawyer and for me of what the day did out here, and what it was like.

FOUR LEAN HOUNDS, CA. 1976

THE FIRST TIME Hank slept with Kay—the only time—was the night her husband drowned. Her husband was his best friend, had been for years. Duncan was a great diver, a crack shot, a good storyteller. He seemed to like being in the world more than most people did. He'd married Kay on the grassy bank of a lake up in the Swan River Valley, and everyone danced barefoot and camped out for the weekend. The way Kay looked at Duncan, it was like he was the whole world. Everyone who saw them knew that.

Hank and Duncan had started an underwater-welding business together, and they worked freelance on hydroelectric dams. In the last week of July, they went down to look for earthquake damage on the Hansen Dam, but it seemed fine.

They kept looking, eighty feet down, where it was so cold Hank's bones ached, and found nothing. Duncan waved him back to the surface, and Hank peeled off his wet suit on the gravel bank, getting the sun on his goose-bumped skin. He stashed all his gear in the VW bus and started making notes for the report, but Duncan didn't come up after him. Finally Hank tugged the cold wet suit on and went back down. He found Duncan at the bottom, weighted down by his belt, staring empty-eyed inside his mask. Hank shouted at him, stupidly, bubbles escaping around his regulator and clouding every-thing, and he looped an arm around Duncan's chest to drag him to the surface. On the bank he pumped his friend's ster-num so hard he felt a rib crack, and forced his own air into the sodden lungs. He kept trying long after he knew Duncan was dead.

They were miles from any town, and Hank didn't know what to do. It was too late for an ambulance. He didn't know if you were supposed to move a body, or where he would take it. He finally left Duncan there, and called the cops from a bait-and-beer store on the highway. His hands were shaking and blue, and the woman at the counter eyed him. He didn't know what to say to his wife, and he couldn't call Kay. The woman at the counter kept watching him, so he left, driving north to Duncan and Kay's cabin as the idea that Duncan was dead sank in. He was dead and Hank had left him alone on the lakeshore, after leaving him alone down below, but now getting to Kay seemed as important as getting back to Duncan.

He found her alone at the cabin, hanging laundry on the line. Their four-year-old, Annie, wasn't there, and Hank was glad. Watching Kay hang the clothes, with the blue mountains in the distance, he felt weirdly calm, as if everything had settled down into a space Duncan didn't occupy anymore, a space that would never be any different than it was now.

Kay didn't cry right away; he had never seen her cry. Duncan used to say Kay's father was the strongest small man he'd ever known, and had never said more than eight words together. Kay was her father's daughter: she hung the last pair of Duncan's jeans, then went inside to call her brother, to ask him to keep Annie for the night.

They drove in silence back to the reservoir, and as they approached they could see Duncan's body next to a police cruiser. One officer snapped pictures while the other sat sideways in the open car door, talking on the radio. Hank wished he had waited to call them, so Kay could have been with Duncan alone. She knelt by the body and pushed her husband's hair from his forehead. Hank answered the cops' questions, feeling awkward and angry. Yes, he had surfaced first, alone. When he found Duncan there had been no pulse, and CPR had failed. He felt the cops' contempt for him, for letting his partner die. Finally they took Duncan away.

The sun was down when they got back to Kay's empty cabin. Hank laid his coat on the table Duncan had made from a cable spool turned on its side, and she pulled the string that turned on the light. Kay was pale and dark-haired, with a thin face and strong hands like a man's. Her eyes were red-rimmed, though she still hadn't cried. Hank had never heard the cabin so quiet. The threading hole in the middle of the table was filled with Annie's stuffed animals and toys. Hank stood there looking at the toys, and Kay stood looking at him, and then he comforted her in the only way that made sense at the time.

She put her arms around his neck, and he lifted her to the tall pine log-frame bed Duncan had built, and he undressed her and held her, still feeling the calm in Duncan's absence that seemed to ring in his ears, until she cried out and clung to him, her body wrapped around his own, and then she began to cry for real. It wasn't the thing he would have chosen to happen, but he felt strangely relieved. They'd broken the dead space Duncan had left behind and it seemed that now things would start changing.

The funeral was in a cemetery so forgotten that it was just a field, grown over with sweetgrass and bitterroot. They'd fought the mortuary to be allowed to take Duncan there themselves, in a pine box loaded in his own pickup truck. Hank helped dig the grave, and the sky threatened rain. His wife, Demeter, was stoned. She was at her worst when she was stoned, and she'd been at her worst a lot in the days since Duncan had died.

After they got the hole dug, Hank opened the door of the VW bus and looked in at Demeter, who'd been crying. "Put your shoes on," he said.

"I can't." Her hiking boots were on the floor, her socked feet tucked up on the seat. She had a hole in the toe of one gray sock.

Hank shut the door and left her there. She'd been singing to herself on the drive up, a song that started "All in green went my love riding." Demeter had a voice on her, but this wasn't one of her songs. Her songs were Texas trail songs, Lone Star laments. The drive to the cemetery had taken a good forty-five minutes, and the whole way she sang, "Four lean hounds crouched low and smiling, the merry deer ran before." She was singing in her low voice; Demeter's low voice meant trouble when she talked, and Hank didn't like hearing her sing in it. But there was no telling Demeter to stop. The song went on and on, and when she seemed to finish she would start over, as if it were all one long song.

Hank thought if Demeter could get her head on straight, she'd be all anyone could want. Long ashy hair, freckled shoulders, Texas in her voice. Her rancher father had named her for the harvest goddess, and stressed the first syllable, like Demerol. She was the first girl who kept Hank's mind from wandering, so he'd tried to keep hers from wandering, too. But lately Demeter had a look in her eye like he'd failed.

Hank opened the tailgate of the pickup, and Duncan's yellow dog Blue jumped in, circled around next to the long pine box and whined a little. More people had arrived from town, and Kay's two brothers helped Hank pull the box off the truck and carry it to the hole in the field, near a low iron fence with grass fields beyond. The box rocked with their different gaits. Kay trailed behind, in jeans and a red rain poncho, with dark-headed Annie in tow.

The coroner had said Duncan's heart had stopped, and he had drowned as a result. He said Hank wasn't to blame, but Hank blamed himself. Kay had always wanted Duncan to stop diving and do something else: take a state job, run for office, raise sheep in their pasture. Sometimes she'd been teasing but mostly she hadn't. The night they saw Duncan dead, she told Hank she couldn't believe it had happened, because she'd worried about it so much; you worried so a thing wouldn't happen, and then it did.

Demeter managed to get her shoes on, and made her way

across the cemetery. Her cotton dress was slipping off her shoulders, and she wore no jacket in the wind. She picked up Annie at the edge of the grave, hugged her to her hip and pushed the girl's dark hair from her eyes. "You look like your daddy," she said.

"Jesus, don't say that," Hank said.

Demeter gave him a slow, sideways, don't-fuck-with-me look. She turned back to Duncan's daughter. "Your daddy will always be inside you," she told her. "You're a little piece of him." She brought the girl's pale cheek to her lips. With her hair loose in the wind, she looked like a painting: Madonna with another woman's child, in a white peasant dress and hiking boots, the fields behind her clean yellow waves. She carried Annie to the other side of the gaping hole.

Kay watched them go. "Annie doesn't understand all this," she said. "Maybe Demeter can explain it better than I can."

"I don't think Demeter understands," Hank said. "I think she's on another planet."

"She understands," Kay said. She shoved her hands in her jeans pockets under the poncho. "At least as much as we do."

Trying to understand had made Hank miserable and afraid. They'd hired a lawyer to investigate the accident, but there was no one to sue except Hank. There wasn't any insurance because they could never afford it; Duncan had always said his luck was insurance enough. Kay was left with nothing, and she was holding up better than he was.

More cars and trucks arrived, dusty from the drive up from town, and people—thirty or forty now—gathered in the field. There was no minister, so everyone looked to Kay to start. She stood near the head of the grave.

"Listen, I know you all loved him," she began. She wrapped her arms around her poncho to hold it down in the wind. "He'd be real glad you all came out." Her face started to screw up and she wiped her hand across her nose. "I don't really know what to say," she said. "So—Annie made a tape yesterday. It's her talking to her dad." She pushed a button on a cassette player, and Annie's four-year-old voice carried over the grave, sounding like she was stuck in a box, but loud enough and clear enough.

"Daddy, we love you," the voice said.

Released by Demeter, Annie dodged through legs to get to Kay, and pressed her face into her mother's thighs. On the tape, you could hear Kay saying something muffled in the background.

"I have my fish, but they're not swimming," the taped Annie said.

"Duncan got her these little plastic fish," Kay explained, stroking her daughter's hair. "Do you hear your voice, sweetie?"

The men moved in to help pick up the pine box, and Hank braced himself to lower it down. It bumped against the edges and he felt concerned for Duncan, then incredulous that Duncan could be inside. On the tape, Annie kept talking about fish. The box touched the bottom and they all looked at it in the hole.

"Oh, God," Kay said.

"I'm going to be a good girl, Daddy," Annie said on the tape.

Kay had a shovel, and she dropped the first dirt on the lid of the coffin. It didn't thud as Hank expected it to; it was dry and loose and fell evenly, like sand. Digging it out was no preparation for hearing it go back in. All the green of spring, the living grass, had been dried out by a month of high-desert sun and wind. Even the summer thunderstorms were gone too quick to bring the green back, or the wetness to the soil.

Kay gave the shovel to Hank and he dropped his portion of dirt on the box. He looked around the crowd, not knowing who should go next.

"I'm going to sing Daddy a song," Annie's taped voice said. She started to sing in her little-girl voice, "All in green went my love riding, on a great horse of gold into the silver dawn."

"I think Duncan must have sung it to her," Kay said. "I think it's a poem."

"Four lean hounds crouched low and smiling, the merry deer ran before," Annie sang on the tape.

Hank still held the shovel in his hand, and Demeter took it from him. She was coming down off her high, he could see, and she was purposeful in taking the shovel, and in dropping the earth into the grave. Hank stepped back from the hole, feeling he might fall in.

Annie, on the tape, sang, "Four red robots at a white water."

Four red roebuck, he corrected her in his mind. He'd thought of hunting season when Demeter sang that line in the car, the season that would be coming soon, and all the past seasons with Duncan. The shorter days, the gloves pulled off to fire a rifle in the wind, the look of a buck as it stared you down, unafraid, then crumpled and fell. The rush of a shot fired well, and the sad feeling of the heavy body that had to be dragged bleeding back to the truck. Now he thought about how you can not know the songs a man sings when he's alone with his little girl, or with your girl.

"Softer be they than slipper-sleep," Annie's voice sang, "the lee lie deer."

Lean lithe deer, Hank thought. He looked around at Duncan's friends, and wondered what they knew.

Kay knelt next to Annie, who held a fistful of dirt and didn't want to let it go. "It's for Daddy," Kay told her. "It's to help Daddy make the flowers grow."

Annie opened her fist and let the dirt spill down the rough wall of the grave. The boxed-up voice stopped, and there was a fuzzy silence. Demeter had sat down on the ground, away from the hole, cross-legged with her elbows on her thighs.

"Maybe you should say something," Kay said to Hank.

She looked at him, waiting. He tried to think what he would have said before. How Duncan was impatient and saw through people and how he was lucky and felt it. How you trusted him because he saw through everyone's bullshit, so well you couldn't believe he had bullshit of his own. But if Hank said any of that now, he was a fool.

"He was my best friend," he started. He looked at Demeter. She didn't look stoned at all anymore, just sad. "He was my best friend, and he was a good man." It sounded sentimental and stupid to him, but he went on.

"He left behind this family," he said, "and I love them and wish he hadn't died." He kept talking even though his head felt like it was somewhere else, maybe on Demeter's planet. "I feel responsible, you know. I guess you all know I was there when he—when it happened. I didn't make him come back up with me, and I didn't wait for him. I was so close, and I didn't know."

Annie's voice came faintly from the tape, singing another song, one Hank didn't know, though he guessed Demeter did. He couldn't say anything more.

Kay stopped the tape player and put a hand on his arm. "Let's all sing something," she said. "Demeter'll start."

The cemetery was quiet except for the wind in the grass, and Demeter stood up where she was, apart from the grave, and started to sing "Home on the Range." It sounded crazy at first, but something in her voice made it sound just right for a funeral. It wasn't the low, ominous voice from the car, but it was clear and slow, and other people joined in. Demeter closed her eyes and sang in that voice that was bigger than she was, and Hank could hear Kay beside him singing, "Where the deer and the antelope play." Even Annie sang, and it seemed good to have a song Annie could sing. Hank didn't feel close to Demeter, exactly—he hadn't felt that in a long time—but he felt something else he hadn't felt in a long time: that Demeter was doing exactly the right thing. A hawk flew overhead, watching them, and all the voices came together, all the people in jeans and boots and windbreakers and dresses, people who loved Duncan and didn't want him in the ground. There was a secretary who always called Duncan "honey," an old uncle and the uncle's daughter, and an ex-girlfriend who looked embarrassed and sad. They were singing, all together, "And the skies are not cloudy all day."

When the song was over there was a silence and everyone looked at one another, then moved toward their cars and trucks, like they knew there wasn't anything more to say.

Hank helped fill in the grave, and thought about Duncan's body in the sun-bleached wet suit on the bank. His arms ached from shoveling, then stopped aching, and when the grave was filled, there were blisters starting on his hands.

Demeter was waiting in the gravel parking lot. He wasn't

sure what he was going to say to her. "Duncan," he finally said.

"He's gone now," Demeter said.

It seemed important to know how long it had been, but it also seemed important not to hear the number of weeks or months or years, not always to have that number in his head. He cleared his throat, but said nothing.

"I just want to get stoned," Demeter said.

"That's my girl," he said, then wished he hadn't. Talking with Demeter had been hard for a while, and now it was going to be harder. Whatever he had felt toward her during the singing was gone.

"I want to get stoned and I want to go home and then I don't know what I want," she said. "I want to go back to Texas."

"There's nothing for you in Texas," he said, but he wasn't sure if that was true. He looked up at the sky, all the rain clouds blown out of it. The hawk was gone.

He said, "He was my best friend," and he didn't know what he was talking about, Duncan's sleeping with his wife or his sleeping with Duncan's, or Duncan's drowning on his watch. He thought again of Duncan's pale face, the sickening feeling of his friend's cold, still mouth under his.

"That didn't make him yours," she said.

Hank shook his head. "Oh, Demeter," he said.

The road wound down into the valley, and there was a thunderstorm coming from the east that might not make it to town: it might hit the mountains and move on, with the wind blowing like it was.

People were going to Kay's cabin, but Hank couldn't stand to sit around that cable-spool table where the four of them had sat so many nights, eating food they'd shot or caught, smoking the communal stash and singing Texas songs to Demeter's guitar. He used to go outside with Demeter after those nights, and if it was winter she'd be wrapped in a shearling jacket with the collar up so her hair bunched out of it like corn silk. He'd have kissed Kay good night, on her smooth bony cheek, and Demeter would have kissed Duncan—years of that—and the sky would be so bright with stars, out where there weren't any lights at all, that it made him dizzy with the bigness of it. Demeter's breath would hang cloudy in the air, and she'd hug her guitar case and laugh, and Hank had felt so lucky on those nights, especially early on—he didn't think any man had ever felt luckier. Duncan said he was born lucky, but Hank had come into luck.

Demeter leaned her head against her window and her eyes flickered at the fence posts and telephone poles going by. There was a load of firewood stacked up on a tarp in the back. It had seemed like a good thing to bring to Kay, and splitting it had taken his mind off the accident. He could forget the lawyers and funeral arrangements and think of the next swing of the ax. The wood was hard and dry and split cleanly; he only had to pry a few logs apart with the blade. If they didn't go to Kay's, he was stuck with the wood. If he went alone, later, nothing would happen between them. He was only a friend to Kay, and their sad awkwardness in the cabin would prove it.

"Let's take her the wood and unload it," Demeter said suddenly, as if she knew what he was thinking. "Then we'll have been there. We don't have to go in the house."

Sometimes the Texas came out in Demeter, not the singing Texas, but the Texas that got things done. At the cabin, three cars were parked in the dirt driveway, and Kay's old aunt carried a covered dish into the house. Hank backed up to the woodpile under the eaves, and Kay came out, drying her hands on a kitchen towel.

"I didn't think you two were coming," she said.

"We brought you some firewood."

"Oh, that's too much," she said. Hank could see her realizing that Duncan wouldn't be around to cut the wood anymore, and he opened the tailgate so he wouldn't have to see that fact take hold on her face.

When he turned back to give Demeter his work gloves, the two women were in each other's arms, holding on tight and dry-eyed, each looking fiercely over the other's shoulder. Hank felt like he shouldn't be there, like he wasn't there: they had no awareness of him. He dropped the gloves, loaded up his arms with wood and tried not to look at the women. Duncan had wronged him, but all he could hate his friend for was that Duncan had been loved. He was on his third armload when they finally let go.

"What would I do without you both?" Kay asked.

Hank thought it might have been better if they'd never met. He said so after Kay went in the house. Demeter looked at him, fine hair down around her shoulders, jacket sleeves hanging loose, hiking boots sticking out below her dress.

"Duncan still would have dived alone," she said. Her nose had started to run, and she held her wrist against it. "Some other woman would've turned his head, and his heart would have done what it did." She shook her head. "Duncan just ran out of luck," she said. "He would have done it with or without us."

Then she turned from him, picked up the work gloves and

put them on. They unloaded the wood slowly, like they were underwater, in silence except for the sharp drop of split logs. As they stacked the pile higher, he could hear Demeter's low voice singing in his head: *four lean hounds crouched low and smiling, my heart fell dead before.*

NATIVE SANDSTONE

THERE WAS NO house yet, just a wellhead where the house would be, under an overturned box to keep the sand out. Clay was building the house, and it would be one to live in for a long time, so they were trying to get everything right. From the passenger seat, Susan watched him wedge the box between the green metal stakes that kept it in place. He climbed into the car and threw the water sample into the backseat.

"Now," he said, and he sat with his hand on the ignition.

"The sandstone," Susan said. She checked her watch, hoping they wouldn't interrupt Albert's dinner.

"Right."

Clay backed the station wagon out onto the flattened grass of the road, past the bare area where the well-digging rig had pulled up all the vegetation. Susan got out and dragged the barbed-wire gate aside, and shook the dust out of her sandals before pulling her feet back in after her.

"So, you'll ask Albert," she said. They drove out on the empty two-lane highway. "You always know what to say to him."

"What's to know?" Clay said.

The wind grew louder through the open window. "I just mean he trusts you," she said. Albert was eighty-three, and he had welcomed them warmly—unlike some of the locals—without suspicion of their intentions; he said he thought the town could use new blood. He liked Clay's photographs and always asked Clay about his picture-taking.

"I wonder if we should take him something," Susan said. "Something he could use." She tried to think what that would be. Not a book; he didn't read. He had read the dictionary page by page growing up on a farm, waiting for the wheat to grow, and he knew all the words, but he said books with stories made him tired. Maybe sheet music; he played guitar in a bluegrass band called the Catfish. A retired ethnologist played banjo and mandolin, the local plumber played fiddle. But she didn't know anything about bluegrass.

"Albert gets along all right," Clay said.

Behind them the water sample rolled to the other side of the car with a thump as they turned off the highway. Susan flipped the visor mirror down to see if there was dust on her face, and pushed her hair behind her ears. Her skin had taken on the color of the desert bluffs, she thought, wrinkled at the corners of her eyes. Clay seemed to be moving in the opposite direction: in spite of the gray in his hair, he looked younger.

They pulled up past Albert's irrigated peach trees and

parked between his sky-blue '65 Ford truck and a washing machine missing all four sidewalls, so only the top and the guts remained. A pile of cut sandstone from the pioneer days, chiseled by pioneer hands, spilled down a slope into the rice grass and knapweed. Susan scanned the pale red blocks, wondering, not for the first time, how much exactly there was, how much might be buried in the lawn and under the visible stone. The stone had once been a schoolhouse. On a pilgrimage to the library in Blanding, Susan had looked up an old sepia photograph of boys in caps and girls in aprons standing before a tidy one-room structure with a peaked roof, the blocks held together by mortar now long eroded.

Clay went first up the porch steps, his hair flattened on one side from camping on the property, his two-day beard speckled with white. She followed, conscious of their empty-handedness, their lack of an offering when one should be made. As Clay pulled open the screen door to knock, he said, "You ask."

"You'll help," she said. Then the door opened.

She was shocked by how much older Albert looked. A padded white brace over his shirt held back both shoulders but didn't keep him upright; he bent at the waist as if to make up for the straightness of his braced spine. His eyes, behind thick glasses, were watery and gray.

"Albert," Susan said, trying not to sound too alarmed.

For a long, awkward moment at the door, Albert seemed not to recognize them. "You're back in town," he said finally, and he gestured them in. He moved a pillow to make room among the songbooks and music catalogs on the couch. Under the pillow, the floral blanket covering the upholstery was torn.

"Guess that's in disrepair," he said, and he sat on a folding chair at a card table stacked with opened and unopened mail. Susan tucked her skirt under her knees and sat on the edge of the easy chair.

"I fell last week," Albert said, his hand on the thick white padding of the brace. "I was on the phone long distance and I started talking—saying words that aren't words. Words I was making up. And then I fell backward and lit on my shoulder." He unbuttoned the top two buttons of his shirt and pulled the fabric off his shoulder, revealing a bruise the color of a black plum from his collarbone halfway down his left arm.

Susan flinched at the sight of the bruised skin, and regretted it. "Oh, Albert," she said.

"Some people were here, I had some people visiting," Albert said. "I don't remember what happened, but they got me to the hospital."

"Do you need anything now?" She wished they had brought something useful—a loaf of bread, a quart of milk— wished Clay were acting even a little sympathetic. The accident was going to make their request difficult. Albert was not what he had been.

"I still cook up big soups like when my brother was alive, so I've got stuff in the freezer," he said. He spoke to Clay, who flipped through a book of bluegrass songs.

Clay closed the book in his lap. "Can you play guitar still?"

"I haven't, but I can play," Albert said, fingering chords in the air with his left hand. "If I could rest this elbow on something. Are we supposed to be playing somewhere?"

"I don't think so, not until you're healed up," Clay said. "The band needs you."

"Well," Albert said. "Yes, I have milk and everything." He waved a wrinkled hand with flat, calloused fingers in Susan's direction. "When my friends came by they brought me milk."

Susan tried to think who the friends would be. "The friends who took you to the hospital?"

Albert looked at her. "I was on the phone when I fell, I was alone."

Susan glanced at Clay. "I'm sorry," she said. "I thought you said friends were visiting."

He stood, frowning, and rummaged through the papers on the card table. "Well, people were here," he said. "I wasn't stuck on my back like a turtle all night." He hobbled, bent over in his brace, into a back room.

Susan whispered to Clay, *"Poor Albert."* She felt like the vultures that soared over the valley in the afternoons.

"Can't find the date the Catfish are playing," Albert said, returning. "Losing my memory. Just ask in town."

There was a pause while he sat back down at the card table. Susan wasn't ready to abandon their purpose but she did wish Clay would ask. Men turned to Clay, they trusted him. He did what he said he would; that was why she had married him. But he also held to what he wouldn't do; he had said *you ask* and he was sticking to it. She edged forward on the easy chair.

"Albert," she said, trying not to sound like she was trying to sound as if it had just occurred to her. "We were wondering about that sandstone in the front yard, if you'd be willing to sell it to us."

Albert looked at her and said nothing.

"I mean, if you want to get rid of it, we'd take it off your hands," she said, with a little open-handed gesture and a shrug.

"The sandstone," Albert said, and he turned to Clay. "Have you talked to Kyle Yazzie lately?" he asked. "Is he going to help you build your house?"

"I think so," Clay said easily, moving the bluegrass book off his lap. "He'll lend us his backhoe, anyway."

It was always the way, she thought: Clay got to make breezy conversation about gear and tackle, and she was stuck with requests and complaints. Kyle Yazzie was on the Navajo tribal council; Clay and Albert would start agreeing about him in a minute. He was a man men liked to agree about.

"You should dig up a garden plot while you've got the backhoe," Albert said.

Clay looked to Susan.

"We're not planting much," she said. "Just desert plants we won't have to water." She was embarrassed; she felt strongly about water use, and native plants choked out by imports, but she didn't like to proselytize. And she knew Albert liked his lawn, and liked the imports; he said Russian olives made good shade trees. "I think we'll grow some peppers," she offered.

"Kyle's a nice young man," Albert said. "Plays a good banjo, too."

"His kids have been out to play on our land," Susan said, cutting off Clay's agreement, and feeling foolish once she had done it. She liked Kyle's boys, who chased each other shouting through the tamarisk. She liked his shy daughters, too; the girls were pretty, and she wondered when they would stray from home, and where they would stray to.

Albert said, "Kyle was helping me with some paperwork, a couple-three weeks ago. I guess I trust him all right. I can't always see the numbers." He shuffled magazines and bills around the card table. "Well, I guess I'll give you that sandstone," he said.

Susan said, "Oh, we'd want to pay you for it."

"It was the old schoolhouse, you know, when the town was settled," Albert said. "It was cut from the massive sandstone around here." He gestured at the bluffs outside the window with the back of one hand. "They built that schoolhouse before they built the church. I always thought the schoolhouse must have been prettier than the church. I never thought it was a pretty church, even when I thought I might get married in it."

The thought of Albert in a morning suit in the boxy Mormon temple made Susan want to laugh. He wasn't a Mormon but didn't dislike them; she had seen him argue genially with two boyish elders at his door. "Who were you going to marry?" she asked.

"Oh, no one in particular," Albert said. "I just thought I might." He said it to Clay, who smiled as if he understood.

"It was a pretty schoolhouse," Susan said. "It's beautiful stone. We want native stone to build with, railroad ties, things that fit in. We thought before we cut new stone we'd look for some that was already in blocks."

Albert stood up to look out at the half-buried stone. "When my brother and I, he's dead now, when we bought this place in sixty-six, that stone was there," he said. "We built this house that year, had it built. I still have things to finish, like the molding on that door." The front door was unvarnished, covered with yellow sticky-note reminders; the doorjamb was painted Sheetrock.

"Works fine like it is," Clay said.

Albert dropped his weight back down in his seat. "I'm

eighty-three, I'm probably not going to finish it," he said, and he looked at the back of his hand on the card table. "Those stairs still need to be carpeted. My brother was going to do that. Other things he was going to do." He stopped. "Yes, okay, I'll give you that sandstone."

"You don't have to sell it if you don't want to," Clay said. "Susan just wants a house that's *authentic*." He grinned at her and she frowned.

Albert said, "My brother and I were going to build a house with that stone in sixty-six and had this built instead. Let's call it tentative. When do you need it?"

"Not till spring, I guess," Susan said, calculating. She didn't want to give him all those months to change his mind, but she had a guilty sense they should give him as much time as he wanted. "We can get it anytime."

"Okay. Tentatively, you can have it." Albert pressed lightly at his bruised shoulder. "I want to think a little more."

"No problem if you change your mind," Clay said.

The three of them walked out on the porch and looked down at the pile of rock.

"We could come get it tomorrow or wait till spring," Susan said, fearing suddenly that Albert would forget the conversation and someone else would take the stone away. The people who brought the milk, or the ones who took him to the hospital—if those were, in fact, different people. "Whatever's best for you."

"*Tomorrow?*" Clay said, looking at their station wagon in the driveway. "I don't know how we'll ever get that stuff out of here."

"Clay's building the house, so we're not on any schedule,"

Susan said from the porch stairs. She said it lightly, to cover her misstep. Of course they weren't ready to get it tomorrow.

"With me building," Clay said, "we might never be ready."

"I'll think some more about it," Albert said. "I won't sell it to anyone else, let's say that. Other people have asked for it over the years, but I always thought I'd get around to using it." He pointed out in the yard. "Look, quail," he said.

A covey of eight birds ran out in a line from behind one of the peach trees.

"The ones with quotation marks on their heads," Susan said. The birds marched toward the tamarisk, seeking cover. "I don't remember what they're called."

"They live out there. I hear them all the time, their call is like this," Albert said. He looked hard at the planks of the porch for a few seconds, then whistled a three-note call. "It sounds like, 'How *are* you, how *are* you,'" he said. "And the answer is like this—" He paused again and whistled.

Susan laughed. "'I'm just *fine,* I'm just *fine,*'" she said.

Albert smiled at her. Clay shook his hand. Susan walked down and leaned over one of the stones in the yard, hands on her knees. Other people had asked for it; they were not the first. But they were the most current. They had the first yes.

"You can see the chisel marks," she called up. "It's not enough for a house, but maybe a wall."

"A foundation," Albert said to Clay on the porch.

"Oh, we don't want to hide it," Clay said. "We want to see it."

"Always thought I'd do something with it."

"You could put some more peach trees in where the rock pile is. I'd help you plant them."

Albert turned from the stone to look at Clay for a moment, his hand across the white brace on his chest.

"You still taking pictures?" Albert asked.

"Yep," Clay said.

Susan said, "You come out to our place when you get more mobile. And don't fall down anymore."

Albert smiled. "Don't plan to." He took off his glasses to clean them on his shirt.

"Think of a price if you decide to sell it," she said. "I don't know how much a rock costs. If we could even have a few of them, that'd be great."

"Well, maybe we can work out a trade," Albert said to Clay.

"Sure," Clay said, and he started down the steps.

"We'll think of something good," Susan called, one hand on the car door, the other shading her eyes from the low, evening sun.

Inside the station wagon, Clay started the old engine. "How am I gonna move those blocks," he said. "Low flatbed trailer, I guess."

"Easier on the chassis," Susan said, and they both were silent. The car was hot, the light no longer pleasant but flat and oppressive. The engine seemed loud as they backed down the drive.

"You wanted it, too, right?" she asked.

"Sure," Clay said. "Just don't know how I'm going to move it."

"You weren't much help," she said. But he'd done all right, and, anyway, they had the stone. "It almost didn't feel worth it," she said. "I thought he knew he wouldn't use it."

"You want to give it back?"

"No. Someone else would just take it."

Clay turned the car around in the clearing by Albert's tool-shed, and the water sample in the back rolled again to the other side of the car, bumping against the door. Susan looked over her shoulder to wave good-bye, but Albert didn't see her. He stood against the porch railing with his glasses in his hand, straight-shouldered in the brace and tilted forward, staring out at the spilled and overgrown jumble of stone, the peach trees beyond, the red bluffs across the river.

Susan took the water bottle in her lap to stop the irritating thumping, then looked out the windshield, away from Albert. "Are you sure he understood?" she asked.

Clay nodded and ran a hand over his rough beard.

"If we think of something really good to do with it," she said, "then it won't be so sad to take it." She closed her eyes and found she couldn't picture the stone as part of a building, only as freestanding monuments on their undeveloped lot, upright versions of the ruin in Albert's yard. A bathroom wall with places for soap and plants but without a bathroom, a garden wall with no garden. With effort, she held those walls in her mind and added a framework around them, a roofed house between the shower wall and the garden. Windows and a door, stucco, visible beams; she constructed the house until they reached the two-lane highway, the stone turning corners and supporting ceilings in her mind.

RANCH GIRL

I F YOU'RE WHITE, and you're not rich or poor but some-where in the middle, it's hard to have worse luck than to be born a girl on a ranch. It doesn't matter if your dad's the fore-man or the rancher—you're still a ranch girl, and you've been dealt a bad hand.

If you're the foreman's daughter on Ted Haskell's Running H cattle ranch, you live in the foreman's house, on the dirt road between Haskell's place and the barn. There are two bed-rooms with walls made of particleboard, one bathroom (no tub), muddy boots and jackets in the living room, and a kitchen that's never used. No one from school ever visits the ranch, so you can keep your room the way you decorated it at ten: a pink comforter, horse posters on the walls, plastic horse models on the shelves. Outside there's an old cow-dog with a ruined hip, a barn cat who sleeps in the rafters, and, until he dies, a runt calf named Minute, who cries at night by the front door.

You help your dad when the other hands are busy: wading after him into an irrigation ditch, or rounding up a stray cow-calf pair when you get home from school. Your mom used to help, too—she sits a horse better than any of the hands—but then she took an office job in town, and bought herself a house to be close to work. That was the story, anyway; she hasn't shown up at the ranch since junior high. Your dad works late now, comes home tired and opens a beer. You bring him cheese and crackers, and watch him fall asleep in his chair.

Down the road, at the ranch house, Ted Haskell grills steaks from his cows every night. He's been divorced for years, but he's never learned how to cook anything except steak. Whenever you're there with Haskell's daughter Carla, who's in your class at school, Haskell tries to get you to stay for dinner. He says you're too thin and a good beefsteak will make you strong. But you don't like Haskell's teasing, and you don't like leaving your dad alone, so you walk home hungry.

When you're sixteen, Haskell's ranch house is the best place to get ready to go out at night. Carla has her own bathroom, with a big mirror, where you curl your hair into ringlets and put on blue eye shadow. You and Carla wear matching Wranglers, and when it gets cold you wear knitted gloves with rainbow-striped fingers that the boys love to look at when they get drunk out on the Hill.

The Hill is the park where everyone stands and talks after they get bored driving their cars in circles on the drag. The cowboys are always out on the Hill, and there's a fight every night; on a good night, there are five or six. On a good night, someone gets slid across the asphalt on his back, T-shirt riding up over his bare skin. It doesn't matter what the fights are about—no one ever knows—it just matters that Andy Tyler always wins. He's the one who slides the other guy into the road. Afterward, he gets casual, walks over with his cowboy-boot gait, takes a button from the school blood drive off his shirt and reads it aloud: "'I Gave Blood Today,'" he says. "Looks like you did, too." Then he pins the button to the other guy's shirt. He puts his jean jacket back on and hides a beer inside it, his hand tucked in like Napoleon's, and smiles his invincible smile.

"Hey," he says. "Do that rainbow thing again."

You wave your gloved hands in fast arcs, fingers together so the stripes line up.

Andy laughs, and grabs your hands, and says, "Come home and fuck me."

But you don't. You walk away. And Andy leaves the Hill without saying good-bye, and rolls his truck in a ditch for the hundredth time, but a buddy of his dad's always tows him, and no one ever calls the cops.

Virginity is as important to rodeo boys as to Catholics, and you don't go home and fuck Andy Tyler because when you finally get him, you want to keep him. But you like his asking. Some nights, he doesn't ask. Some nights, Lacey Estrada climbs into Andy's truck, dark hair bouncing in soft curls on her shoulders, and moves close to Andy on the front seat as they drive away. Lacey's dad is a doctor, and she lives in a big white house where she can sneak Andy into her bedroom without waking anyone up. But cowboys are romantics; when they settle down they want the girl they haven't fucked.

When Haskell marries an ex-hippie, everyone on the ranch expects trouble. Suzy was a beauty once; now she's on her third husband and doesn't take any shit. Suzy reads tarot cards, and when she lays them out to answer the question of Andy Tyler, the cards say to hold out for him.

On the spring cattle drive, you show Suzy how to ride behind the mob and stay out of the dust. Suzy talks about her life before Haskell: she has a Ph.D. in anthropology, a police record for narcotics possession, a sorority pin and a ski-bum son in Jackson Hole. She spent her twenties throwing dinner parties for her first husband's business clients—that, she says, was her biggest mistake—and then the husband ran off with one of her sorority sisters. She married a Buddhist next. "Be interesting in your twenties," Suzy says. "Otherwise you'll want to do it in your thirties or forties, when it wreaks all kinds of havoc, and you've got a husband and kids."

You listen to Suzy and say nothing. What's wrong with a husband and children? A sweet guy, a couple of brown-armed kids running around outside—it wouldn't be so bad.

There's a fall cattle drive, too, but no one ever wants to come on it. It's cold in November, and the cows have scattered in the national forest. They're half wild from being out there for months, especially the calves, who are stupid as only calves can be. The cowboys have disappeared, gone back to college or off on binges or other jobs. So you go out with your dad and Haskell, sweating in heavy coats as you chase down the calves, fighting the herd back to winter pasture before it starts to snow. But it always snows before you finish, and your dad yells at you when your horse slips on the wet asphalt and scrapes itself up.

In grade school, it's okay to do well. But by high school, being smart gives people ideas. Science teachers start bugging you in the halls. They say Eastern schools have Montana quotas, places for ranch girls who are good at math. You could get scholarships, they say. But you know, as soon as they suggest it, that if you went to one of those schools you'd still be a ranch girl—not the Texas kind, who are debutantes and just happen to have a ranch in the family, and not the horse-farm kind, who ride English. Horse people are different, because horses are elegant and clean. Cows are mucusy, muddy, shitty, slobbery things, and it takes another kind of person to live with them. Even your long curled hair won't help at a fancy college, because prep-school girls don't curl their hair. The rodeo boys like it, but there aren't any rodeo boys out East. So you come up with a plan: you have two and a half years of straight A's, and you have to flunk quietly, not to draw attention. Western Montana College, where Andy Tyler wants to go, will take anyone who applies. You can live cheap in Dillon, and if things don't work out with Andy you already know half the football team.

When rodeo season begins, the boys start skipping school. You'd skip, too, but the goal is to load up on D's, not to get kicked out or sent into counseling. You paint your nails in class and follow the rodeo circuit on weekends. Andy rides saddle bronc, but his real event is bull riding. The bull riders have to be a little crazy, and Andy Tyler is. He's crazy in other ways, too: two years of asking you to come home and fuck him have made him urgent about it. You dance with him at the all-night graduation party, and he catches you around the waist and says he doesn't know a more beautiful girl. At dawn, he leaves for spring rodeo finals in Reno, driving down with his best friend, Rick Marcille, and you go to Country Kitchen for breakfast in a happy fog, order a chocolate shake and think about dancing with Andy. Then you fall asleep on Carla's bedroom floor, watching cartoons, too tired to make it down the road to bed.

Andy calls once from Reno, at 2 A.M., and you answer the phone before it wakes your dad. Andy's taken second place in the bull riding and won a silver belt buckle and three thousand dollars. He says he'll take you to dinner at the Grub Stake when he gets home. Rick Marcille shouts "Ro-*day*-o" in the background.

There's a call the next night, too, but it's from Rick Marcille's dad. Rick and Andy rolled the truck somewhere in Idaho, and the doctors don't think Rick will make it, though Andy might. Mr. Marcille sounds angry that Andy's the one who's going to live, but he offers to drive you down there. You don't wake your dad; you just go.

The doctors are wrong; it's Andy who doesn't make it. When you get to Idaho, he's already dead. Rick Marcille is paralyzed from the neck down. The cops say the boys weren't drinking, that a wheel came loose and the truck just rolled, but you guess the cops are just being nice. It's your turn to be angry, at Mr. Marcille, because his son will live and Andy is dead. But when you leave the hospital, Mr. Marcille falls down on his knees, squeezing your hand until it hurts.

At Andy's funeral, his uncle's band plays, and his family sets white doves free. One won't go, and it hops around the grass at your feet. The morning is already hot and blue, and there will be a whole summer of days like this to get through.

Andy's obituary says he was engaged to Lacey Estrada, which only Lacey or her doctor father could have put in. If you had the guts, you'd buy every paper in town and burn them outside the big white house where Lacey took him home and fucked him. Then Lacey shows up on the Hill with an engagement ring and gives you a sad smile as if you've shared something. If you were one of the girls who gets in fights on the Hill, you'd fight Lacey. But you don't; you just look away. You'll all be too old for the Hill when school starts, anyway.

At Western, in the fall, in a required composition class, your professor accuses you of plagiarism because your first paper is readable. You drop the class. Carla gets an A on her biology midterm at the university in Bozeman. She's going to be a big-animal vet. Her dad tells everyone, beaming.

But the next summer, Carla quits college to marry a boy named Dale Banning. The Bannings own most of central Montana, and Dale got famous at the family's fall livestock sale. He'd been putting black bulls on Herefords, when everyone wanted purebreds. They said he was crazy, but at the sale Dale's crossbred black-baldies brought twice what the purebreds did. Dale stood around grinning, embarrassed, like a guy who'd beaten his friends at poker.

Carla announces the engagement in Haskell's kitchen, and says she'll still be working with animals, without slogging through all those classes. "Dale's never been to vet school," Carla says. "But he can feel an embryo the size of a pea inside a cow's uterus."

You've heard Dale use that line on girls before, but never knew it to work so well. Carla's voice has a dreamy edge.

"If I don't marry him now," Carla says, "he'll find someone else."

In his head, Haskell has already added the Banning acreage to his own, and the numbers make him giddy. He forgets about having a vet for a daughter, and talks about the wedding all the time. If Carla backed out, he'd marry Dale himself. For the party, they clear the big barn and kill a cow. Carla wears a high-collared white gown that hides the scar on her neck—half a Running H—from the time she got in the way at branding, holding a struggling calf. Dale wears a string tie and a black ten-gallon hat, and everyone dances to Andy's uncle's band.

Your mother drives out to the ranch for the wedding; it's the first time you've seen your parents together in years. Your dad keeps ordering whiskeys and your mother gets drunk and giggly. But they sober up enough not to go home together.

That winter, your dad quits his job, saying he's tired of Haskell's crap. He leaves the foreman's house and moves in with his new girlfriend, who then announces he can't stay there without a job. He hasn't done anything but ranch work for twenty-five years, so he starts day-riding for Haskell again, then working full-time hourly, until he might as well be the foreman.

When you finish Western, you move into your mother's house in town. Stacks of paperwork for the local horse-racing board cover every chair and table, and an old leather racing saddle straddles an arm of the couch. Your mother still thinks of herself as a horsewoman, and buys unbroken Thoroughbreds she doesn't have time or money to train. She doesn't have a truck or a trailer, or land for pasture, so she boards the horses and they end up as big, useless pets she never sees.

Summer evenings, you sit with your mom on the front step and eat ice cream with chocolate-peanut-butter chunks for dinner. You think about moving out, but then she might move in with you—and that would be worse.

You aren't a virgin anymore, thanks to a boy you found who wouldn't cause you trouble. He drops by from time to time, to see if things might start up again. They don't. He's nothing like Andy. He isn't the one in your head.

When Carla leaves Dale and moves home to the Running H, you drive out to see her baby. It feels strange to be at the ranch now, with the foreman's house empty and Carla's little boy in the yard, and everything else the same.

"You're so lucky to have a degree and no kid," Carla says. "You can still leave."

And Carla is right: You could leave. Apply to grad school in Santa Cruz and live by the beach. Take the research job in Chicago that your chemistry professor keeps calling about. Go to Zihuatanejo with Haskell's friends, who need a nanny. They have tons of room, because in Mexico you don't have to pay property tax if you're still adding on to the house.

But none of these things seem real; what's real is the payments on your car and your mom's crazy horses, the feel of the ranch road you can drive blindfolded and the smell of the hay. Your dad will need you in November to bring in the cows.

Suzy lays out the tarot cards on the kitchen table. The cards say, Go on, go away. But out there in the world you get old. You don't get old here. Here you can always be a ranch girl. Suzy knows. When Haskell comes in wearing muddy boots, saying, "Hi, baby. Hi, hon," his wife stacks up the tarot cards and kisses him hello. She pours him fresh coffee and puts away the cards that say go.

GARRISON JUNCTION

IT HAD BEEN snowing hard for twenty-four hours and the snow stayed where it fell. A few cars crawled the streets, white lights emerging from whiteness, red taillights invisible until they were just ahead. The whole valley was socked in, the mountains invisible in the steady snow. Gina left the car running in the driveway with the heat on, and white flakes stung her eyes and melted on her cheeks. It would be worse up on the pass, where the snow came harder.

The phone was ringing inside the house, and the woman on the line asked for Chase. She said her name was Kathleen Sheehan and she was calling about a check; she said Chase would understand. Gina took down the Missoula number, put it in her pocket and went to the bathroom. Her bladder seemed to have shrunk to the size of a walnut. When she stood she felt shaky on her feet.

Chase came in, stomping his boots clean at the door. "How's your car running?" he asked. He had put off getting studded tires on his truck all fall, and no garage in town had time for him now. Gina had put hers on when the roads were still dry.

"I think we should wait out the storm," she said.

"Can't wait." He gathered a stack of manila folders and yellow pads for his deposition, his bare hands red from the cold. Gina wondered, watching him, if Kathleen Sheehan was a client—but then she wouldn't be asking about a check, she'd be explaining why she hadn't sent one.

Chase slid back the driver's seat of Gina's car as he climbed in, and lowered the seatback until he could see out the windshield. Gina buckled her seat belt over her queasy stomach. There were no cars on the valley road, and no cars coming from the mountains, only the snow blowing against the glass and the half-buried tracks ahead. A temporary orange sign posted where the road began to climb said: EMERGENCY VEHICLES ONLY.

"Chase," she said.

"This *is* an emergency," Chase said.

Gina supposed it was an emergency for her, too. She was going to visit her mother while Chase had his deposition, to try to explain. She hadn't slept since she told her mother she was pregnant, and the long nights were worse than the sick mornings, the dark patches flowering like bruises under her eyes. Her mother had said, "So you're going to be a whore like the rest of us." Her mother wasn't well, she knew that, but still she had sat up that night and thought about those women, her mother and grandmother, her lonely aunts, their absent men. Going to college and teaching school had seemed to put her in a separate category from them. No one was marrying when she met Chase—marrying mattered only to her mother, and life with him was good. No reason to change it, no need to.

Now it was ten years later, and the most militant of her college friends had tied various kinds of knots in courtrooms and churches and meadows. A wrongful-termination case in Missoula had brought on two bad years, when Chase was gone all the time, staying nights in a motel instead of driving home. Gina wasn't sure they had made it out of those years intact. She had seen the baby as a happy accident after Chase won his case, drunk on wine and praise, but Chase just saw it as an accident. And now there was Kathleen Sheehan on the phone.

The more immediate fear, as they drove up the winding road to the top of the pass, was that Chase would miss one of the invisible turns and they would go over the invisible edge and plummet to the valley below. The thick curtain of snow parted only a few feet in front of them, and Chase drove slowly, for him, into that curtain, following the disappearing tracks around each curve. The insides of the windows iced, and when she scraped the glass her own frozen breath showered her.

"This is crazy," Gina said.

"I could drive this road blind," Chase said.

There was still no visibility at the top of the pass, only the feeling of going down instead of up. Down was worse; the snow on the road had started to freeze into ice, and their wheels slid until the studded snow tires caught and held, slid and caught again. When the police roadblock stopped them in Garrison Junction in the valley below, Gina's hand was cramped from gripping the door handle, and they hadn't spoken for miles.

"How'd you get through?" the highway patrolman asked when Chase rolled down his frosted window. "That's emergency vehicles only."

"This *is* an emergency," Chase said. It was less convincing when he said it to the cop.

"Well, you can't go through," the officer said. There were white spots on his red cheeks, the beginnings of frostbite. "Road's closed both ways now. There's an accident ahead—a semi stretched out across the highway. No one's getting through today. You can wait in the café until the storm quits and we can get you back home."

They parked at the low-roofed white building with the sign for motel cabins, next to the single-pump gas station. Gina thought about the phone message, about mentioning it while they were still alone, but instead she got out into the storm.

The café was steamy inside with bodies, the linoleum slick with melted snow. Although the room was packed, it wasn't loud. Everyone seemed trapped and tired of it, no giddiness of adventure in the hum of their voices. Gina shook off her boots on the wet rubber mat and dodged the tables to the bathroom, where the roll of toilet paper had fallen into the melted snow on the floor.

When she came out again, a man stepped from the men's door opposite: tall with a dark mustache, in a heavy denim jacket with a dirty sheepskin collar. He looked her in the eye and hesitated, as if he wanted to say something, and then he moved on.

Chase had found two seats at a table by the window, next to

an old man and an old woman with hard-worn faces, and Gina sat down.

"Jesus, I never seen anything like that," the old man was saying. He rubbed chapped hands over eyes gadrooned with wrinkles. His hair was bushy and white, and he had a truck-stop gimme cap on the table.

"We were going west right behind the semi," his wife said, voice low. "A car stopped on the road ahead because they couldn't see, and the semi piled right into them. Killed the man and the woman in the car. We ended up in the ditch to miss the wreck." The woman dropped her voice further. "The driver of the semi's here," she said. She cast her eyes to the center of the crowded room.

Gina knew who it would be, and waited until Chase had looked, then turned to see the tall man with the dirty sheepskin who had given her the hard look by the bathrooms. He sat alone at a small table, drinking coffee. He caught her eye and she nodded at him, feeling awkward, and looked away.

"Just killed two people," the old man said under his breath. "Poor sucker. I don't know how he stands it in here."

Gina thought of the couple in the car, so afraid of what was in front of them that they had forgotten what would be behind. She wondered if they'd been fighting about the road, if they'd argued about what to do, or if they'd agreed to stop. She thought of the view from the truck, the car materializing in the field of white.

"That must be what truckers fear, hitting someone," she said.

The old man widened his eyes. "You ever talk to those guys?" he asked. "We used to run a truck stop in Choteau. Those guys aren't scareda anything."

"Oh, Al, that's not true," his wife said.

"It is."

Chase gazed across the room. "You think they'll get that truck off the road today?"

"Not likely," the old man said. "Not in this storm."

Chase seemed to be thinking. His eyes, downturned at the corners, always seemed to be thinking—not plotting, just considering. She thought it was why juries liked him. Her mother had liked him, too, at first, and liking him might have carried the day with her, except she didn't trust any man at all. Gina's father had pushed her down the stairs when she was twenty, and everyone said the fall had left her a little off. Gina touched the piece of paper through her jeans, felt it crinkle. Finally Chase sighed, and pushed himself to his feet.

"I better go call the judge, then," he said. "Say I'm not coming."

Gina watched him go, past the table where the truck driver sat alone, to the line for the pay phone on the wall. She thought about calling her mother, but her mother wouldn't be expecting her yet. If she called now she would worry.

"You feeling okay, honey?" Al's wife asked her. "You look pale."

Al's wife had the dried-up look of long winters in smoky truck stops, and Gina thought she must look pretty rough to alarm her. But there was concern in the woman's voice, and Gina was grateful for it.

"I guess I don't feel so good," Gina said.

"What're you going on your guy's trip for if you don't feel good?"

Gina held her hands in her lap and knew by the word "guy"

that their ringlessness had been noted. "I was going to visit my mother," she said.

Chase always said Gina was not her mother, but sometimes Gina had to be in the same room with her to make sure they were not the same person and she would not end up damaged, jobless and alone. Gina had started scanning the classifieds for waitressing jobs again—a compulsion, after ten years of teaching, but just to be sure.

"I'm Alice," the woman said. "We were going to see our daughter. Maybe our daughter can get together with your mother." She laughed. "I think your mother'd be disappointed if she got our daughter instead of you."

"I don't know about that," Gina said.

"You don't know our daughter."

"Now," the woman's husband said.

Chase came back to the table. "Can't get through," he said. "That line is all people trying the phone and finding out they can't get through. But they don't tell each other it doesn't work. Or if they do, everyone still wants to try it." He shook his head and sat down.

Gina stood. "I'm going for a hot chocolate," she said. "What can I get you?"

They all asked for coffee and Gina stepped over two children in snowsuits playing on the slushy floor. The waitress at the counter seemed too nice and too old to be a waitress, and Gina talked to her about the snow. When the coffees were ready, Gina felt the truck driver looking at her, and she carried the tray to the table, avoiding his eyes. She thought again of the couple in the car, braking in the road, unable to keep moving forward in the blinding snow. She wondered how soon they had noticed it coming, if they had seen the lights first or heard the shrieking brakes, and who noticed it first, and what they said.

"You're pregnant, aren't you?" Alice asked, nodding at the cup of chocolate. "You seem like a coffee drinker. And you've got the morning-sickness eyes."

"It's that bad, huh?" Gina said.

"Our Shelley's pregnant," Alice said, and she looked at Al as if daring him to say something. "She looks like she got punched in both eyes, too."

"Congratulations," Chase said.

"You, too," Al said. He clapped Chase on the shoulder. "I hope it's a fine kid you get."

Chase looked down at his hands. "I hope so, too."

Al and Alice would see his demeanor as modest and pleased, but Gina guessed Chase was thinking of the burden the baby would be to him, the drain on his time and sleep and money.

Al said, "I gotta move my knee a little." He shoved his chair back with a linoleum squeal, straightened with his hands on his thighs and lumbered away from the table.

"Don't mind him," Alice said.

"Nothing to mind," Chase said easily.

"Now," Alice said. "Why don't you marry this girl?"

Chase raised his eyebrows at Gina.

"I didn't—" Gina began, and she looked at the woman. "What do you mean?"

"No reason why not to," Alice said. "Or is there?"

Chase smiled at Alice, looked out the window and yawned a little self-conscious yawn. "Well, maybe I will," he said. "No reason why not to."

Gina pressed the paper message against her thigh again, a motion that had already become a habit, the feeling of wanting to touch it detached in her mind from what it might mean. Chase would have an explanation for Kathleen Sheehan, for the call. He always did. He would say Gina had to start trusting him someday. But his embarrassed yawn made her angry; the old woman had caught him off-guard, and that was hard to do. Gina heard herself speak.

"Someone called this morning, I forgot to tell you," she said. "A woman."

Chase looked at her, and she could feel him grow alert. "What woman?"

She took the piece of paper from her pocket and read out what she knew by heart. Chase kept the guarded look on his face for a second longer and then laughed. There was relief in his laugh, but Gina didn't know if he was relieved the woman was not who he'd thought, or relieved that once again he had a good answer.

"Katy Sheehan," he said. "Sure. She took some pictures for me, up in the Bitterroot, for a water-rights case. I sent her a check for them." He smiled as if he'd won.

Gina waited.

Alice said, "Why's she asking about the check, then?"

"I don't know," Chase said, serious now. "Come to think of it, I don't think I ever got those pictures."

The old man came back and sat down heavily, ignoring the silence at the table. "Phone's still out," he said.

The windows were fogged and the room was close and warm. Gina believed Chase about the check, but believing him didn't help. It just meant it was true she would have to start trusting him someday. "I'm going to walk around," she said. Her legs were less shaky now, and she stood, leaving the hot chocolate on the table. Alice had guessed right: she missed coffee.

One of the children in snowsuits had fallen asleep under his parents' table; the other played tic-tac-toe with her father in the gray borders of his newspaper. A teenaged girl slept against the wall beneath a print of a bugling elk, and her boyfriend slept with his head on the table, holding her hand. People without tables sat in mismatched chairs pulled from the motel cabins. The line for the phone was gone; everyone had accepted the downed lines and given up. The road back over the pass would open soon, and they could go home, and Gina would call then. She would not have seen her mother but she would have tried. And they would be safe at home, alive and whole.

Gina walked the perimeter of the room once, and when she looked up the driver was watching her. He swung the dregs in his coffee cup in small circles, then put down the cup and stood to go. The people around him looked up. At Gina's shoulder he brushed against her and paused, again as if to say something, then pushed open the fogged glass door and walked out into the snow. She felt the cold air on her throat. The bell tied to the hydraulic arm jingled as the door swung shut, and the room was close and warm again. The people who had watched the driver stand returned to their low conversations or their naps.

Gina went to the door and rubbed a clear spot in the pane. The driver had no truck, and there was nothing but the one-pump gas station out there. The blue denim jacket headed neither toward the gas station nor toward the police roadblock, but straight for the empty road. A cigarette burned in his hand. He would be invisible in the snow in a minute. She put up her hood and stepped outside, the air cold and bright in her lungs, the snow blowing against her face, and she could smell the smoke he left behind. On the other side of the highway were mountains, invisible now but leading, she knew, straight up into the white sky. She watched the dark jacket disappear into white, and then the legs that carried it, until the figure had vanished in the storm.

She shoved her hands in her pockets to keep them warm. She could find the frostbitten policeman and tell him the driver had wandered off. She could follow and see if she could find the man, though it was cold, and he was far away, and what would she say to him? She could tell Chase he was gone; Chase would have an idea about what to do. Or she could just let the driver go, and walk where he wanted. He might be accountable in some way, but no one could say the accident was his fault. Her face was wet and tingling with snow, and the smell of his smoke was gone. She wanted, with an unexpected force, for him to come back. But she imagined feeling what she'd seen in his eye, and what it might be like to walk away, and she went back inside, and let him go.

RED

THERE WERE LINES for everything. Lines for the movies, for telephones, for the bus, lines to piss, lines to eat. The movies were all war glory and girls you couldn't have, the telephones never worked, the buses were crowded, the toilets were filthy, food was scarce and often spoiled, and for all of it people stood to wait. But now Red's troop, holed up in south London, was waiting to be sent to France, where waiting was the least of anyone's problems.

Lying on his bunk, Red wrote his kid sister Jackie about going to France, and then he told her about the lines, the orderly, sad-looking people in gray, and how rotten everything was they waited for. He drew her a cartoon of gloomy, queued-up Brits and hoped Jackie would laugh, but the cartoon made him sad. He never wrote anything about the war or the bombs. Nothing he had to say would get past the censors, and he didn't want to see it on paper. His sister was a sweet kid, half in love with him since he'd become a soldier, a bright, solid American girl. He missed American girls. He missed America. Ranger training in the Florida swamps had been a brutal game, but still a game. He had been good at it, and proud to be a soldier, but here in Southfields it was different. The makeshift barracks stank, and the men stayed out all night with whores and returned in the morning, stinking worse. Red was the only one in the outfit who still had the first issue of condoms; everything to do with sex depressed him too much.

He wrote to his sister, "I miss you like mad—mad like crazy." And then he signed off and took the letter down to the mail desk. He added a postscript while he waited: "Am now waiting in line to mail this. Of course. I will have enormous heavy feet when you see me next, like someone dipped in concrete to be dumped in a river. Feet for waiting in line forever." The officer at the desk read his letter, smirked and sealed the envelope, letting it all go through, and Red went out to find something to eat.

He considered the line waiting along the brick wall of a corner restaurant with blacked-out windows. At the end of the line was a girl. Big eyes, pale skin, a regal neck crowned with piled-up dark hair. A red coat tied at the waist, and high boots. Red joined the line behind her, leaned against the rough brick wall, and was content to look. She required nothing of him, no more than a fine painting required speech or action, but then she turned to him, and the tremendous eyes found his.

"Do you think we'll be here long?" she asked.

Red pushed himself to standing. "No longer than usual."

She didn't turn away. He gathered courage: "Are you hungry?"

She nodded.

"Will you join me?" he asked. "I'm hungry, too." It wasn't a brilliant line, but she didn't seem to care.

"All right," she said.

She had a way of speaking without moving the muscles in her face, as if any contortion of her features would mar them. It annoyed Red, and made him anxious to see such a contortion. Still, it made him happy that to the waitress they must seem like a couple. He held the girl's chair at their table, and she lowered her body into it, straight-backed. She wore a black wool dress under her red coat. He asked what brought her to this part of town, and she looked at the blackened window as if to see what part she was in.

"I was shopping," she said.

"You don't have any shopping bags."

"I couldn't find anything I wanted." She seemed to mean it in a grander sense. "Someone told me about a shop in Wimbledon. But you need to know someone to get anything. Men think stockings are a luxury, but you've never worn a skirt in the cold."

"Never assume," Red said, and a flicker of a smile crossed her face, then vanished. She frowned at the menu, and Red was as grateful for the frown as for the smile—two quick ripples on the surface.

"Are you sad about something?" he asked. "Besides stockings."

"Do I look sad?"

"Are you in love?"

"No." Her voice was nice but careful: a voice to keep people at bay. A waitress came, and the girl asked for soup. Red ordered the same, too distracted for the menu, and asked the girl's name, which was Irene.

"You don't look like an Irene," he said.

"What do I look like?"

"Sandra, or Sonia, or Zelda. Irene is a different girl."

"People mistake me for Spanish," she said.

"No, not Spanish. Russian. A Russian beauty."

"I don't look Russian." Her skin's milky surface had a hint of pink beneath it, and he could guess how the piled-up hair would fall around her shoulders if she let it down.

"It's no insult," Red said. He took pictures from his wallet of sweet Vera back home. "That's a Russian girl," he said.

Vera was as American as they came, but she was beautiful, and might pass for Russian. They'd been useful to each other, and she was useful even now, doing time as a Russian girl.

"She's good-looking," Irene said. She picked up another picture. "This is lovely."

Red studied it. His sister Jackie, at nine or ten, wore his father's tweed cap sideways, tilting her head in the direction of the brim. She smiled, closemouthed and knowing, straight at the camera. "My sister," Red said, and his voice caught on the words.

The soup came, and he tucked the photographs away. "How many men have fallen in love with you?" he asked.

"I don't know."

He studied her, and wondered what it would take to make his sister into a girl this reserved. Was it just the war? It was hard to imagine a war like this at home, the bombs blowing out doorsteps in Biloxi and whole buildings in New York.

"How many men are still in love with you right now?"

"I don't know," she said. She didn't blush, or appear to calculate.

"You're a beautiful girl."

"Really?" Her forehead wrinkled, then smoothed. She lifted her spoon and cooled the soup deliberately before bringing it to her lips.

Red thought about the lines of gray people outside. This girl was dark and light, rose skin and pink lips; it was worth his while to stay in this game, to get past her guard.

"Do you like being beautiful?"

"It's better than not being, I suppose." There was almost a shrug in her voice. Red felt a small, bright victory at provoking it.

"You suppose," he said. He couldn't keep from laughing. "I've never met anyone like you," he said. "You're either the smartest or the dumbest girl I've ever known."

She looked at him. "Is that nice?"

Red pushed the weak soup away. "I give up," he said. "Let's go." He was only half surprised that she followed. It was his last night as a man who'd been good at his training in Florida. In the morning he'd be a man who was at war.

The night was clear, cool in the absence of clouds, moonless and starry in the blackout, and the air improved Red's mood. The waiting lines had dispersed into walking people, single and in pairs, and the people didn't seem so sad in the dark. There had been no bombs for three days, and spirits were high. With Irene beside him, he crossed the Thames at Putney Bridge and the water ran darkly beneath. The night was beautiful, the girl was beautiful, Red himself felt beautiful.

Overcome, he caught the girl's hand in his, but it was so

lifeless and passive it made him angry. He crushed it in his grip, sliding the bones and sinews inward toward the palm, the slender fingers crossing one over the other.

"Don't," the girl said. She pulled her hand from his but kept walking by his side, eyes straight ahead.

"You're like death," Red said. "There's no life in you. What's the point of being beautiful?"

She stopped, and looked ready to answer, but shook her head and began to walk again. He caught her then, and kissed her hard. Her hair smelled like lilacs but her skin smelled like nothing; there was no close body scent to distinguish her from the cold night air. He let her go, and thought he saw some rising expression on her face, but again it went away. Her lips were smeared. She started walking, as if nothing had happened. He caught her and matched her pace.

She said, without looking at him, "You're passionate, I guess."

He felt the arteries in his neck distend in anger. He would walk her home and be done with it. With the streetlamps out, he had to be careful not to trip. He listened to the hollow click of her square heels, the thud of his own.

"You can stay with me if you like," she said.

He stopped on the pavement, intending that she stop also, but she kept on, and he ran a few steps to keep up with her.

"You mean I can share your bed?" he said.

"Yes," she said. "If you like."

Red laughed, but he had to think about the proposition, and he frowned to himself, hands stuffed in his pockets. To look at her, she was worth a lot—worth saying what the hell. But it made him sick to think of her blank face afterward on the pillow, her even voice saying, "Are you finished?" It was the girls in his head who'd got him this far: the images from movies, the thought of sweet Vera, the letters from his sister. This girl could poison all that; he couldn't take the chance.

"Well, I don't," he said finally. "I don't like."

Irene didn't seem angry, but said good night on the steps of her rooming house. Red didn't kiss her again. He walked back alone in the direction from which they had come, and every few steps he stomped his foot and swung one arm to strike at the air. He'd been cruel to her, and yet he was in. There was no play in it, no beauty. He wanted to go back to America, to soft girls on porches, and blouses wet from dancing, and the old fight over who belonged to whom, or if anyone belonged to anyone. Instead he was going to France, and he'd be lucky to get there alive.

He swung his arm at the air again, and stomped, then turned and half ran, half walked back to her rooming house. He knocked, though it was late, and an old woman came to the door.

"I'd like to talk to that girl, Irene," he said. "I'm shipping out in the morning and it's very important."

The woman let him in, to his surprise, and left him in the foyer while she knocked on a downstairs door. The girl emerged at the end of the hallway with her hand on the door frame for support, sidelit by the yellow light from her room. She still wore the black dress, but the red coat was gone and she looked smaller standing there, her shoulders less queenly-proud. The old woman disappeared.

He'd meant to tell the girl about the movies he'd seen with the men in Ranger training, when they'd crawled around in the swamps without a girl in sight for days, then found themselves in a dark room with Lana Turner begging for love. He wanted to tell her about men's desire—his own desire—and how little came in return for it sometimes. He thought, there in the rooming-house hallway, he had some important point to make, but now he didn't know what the point was, and couldn't find the words he meant to say.

The girl's eyes were red from crying she must have controlled before opening the door. In the little room she had offered to share with him, he took her pale face in his hands, and it was warm. He hadn't felt that warmth when he had kissed her so roughly on the street.

"I have a sister," he said.

"I know," the girl said. Her eyes were lost-looking and plaintive now.

"She's a sweet kid," he said.

"I could be sweet like her," Irene said, and she dipped her face toward his hand.

"Oh, don't do that," he said. "Don't say that."

He looked around the little room. There was a knitted afghan over the foot of the single bed, a needlepoint pillow on a rocking chair, a bureau topped by a mirror leaning against the wall, the mirror spotty where the silver had worn away. A homely room that didn't match her.

"Why do you live here alone?" he asked.

"What if I said I don't?"

"No one else lives here," he said.

She looked toward the spotty mirror. "They killed my husband," she said, "and I went to live with my granny, and they bombed her house, and she died in hospital." She looked back at him, her eyes drawn and tired. "And now I live here."

Red felt a quick glandular surge, a desire to avenge her, and it was like the movies: blood-stirring patriotism and a girl he couldn't have. But he could have her. But he didn't want her; it all made him too sad. And he couldn't avenge her. All he could do was try not to get killed. He took her hand. "Come out here," he said. "No—get your coat first. We shouldn't be in your room."

She put on the red coat and tied it around her waist and they sat on the front steps outside the rooming house. The stone was cold through Red's thin trousers, and he sat on his hands until it warmed up. The stars were bright with the street-lamps dark, and no one walked by. They sat a long time saying nothing, and then the girl lay back on the hard stoop and put her hands behind her head like a pillow, and Red did the same.

"I'm going to France in the morning," he said, after a while. It surprised him to think she didn't already know.

She looked over at him. She was close enough to kiss if he sat up a little, but he didn't want that. He just wanted her lying there. Her eyes were solemn.

"It's going to be worse than you know," she said.

Red looked back up at the sky. A mist had drifted in, obscuring the stars, which had moved some distance along their course, and soon the waiting would be over. After a while the girl moved her hand from behind her head and took Red's in hers, and they lay on the chill stone like an old couple in an old bed, fingers intertwined, until the sky began to lighten, and it was time for Red to go.

AQUA BOULEVARD

Each day I walk to the Polo Club, while my wife is at work and my children at school. I have my lunch at the club, a little wine, and I walk home. I don't work anymore; I worked long enough, and very hard. I could have a horse at the club, well groomed and cared for. I would not get any better, at my age, but I could ride. But I like only to ride in the country—going somewhere—not in a hall in the middle of Paris, going in circles. I would rather walk. So I walk to my lunch, I watch the horses, I walk back.

Last week at the Polo I saw a woman I knew. She would not have been allowed before: she is a black woman, from Martinique. But the club now lets many people in, and she was an actress in films for some years. I knew her when she was young; her husband and I were like brothers. It was strange to see her that day at the club because she had not changed in thirty years. She was still beautiful, still sexy. A bright girl, with energy. I remember her always laughing, swinging her legs on the dock at Cap-Ferrat, or sitting on a boat or in a café, but always laughing, showing the gap between her front teeth. She was not laughing so much this time, but when she did it was the same laugh, the same gap. She had the good skin of black women, the face and hands still young. She called herself Mia. We watched her granddaughter do vaultige: the girl stood on the back of the horse at a *petit galop* around the ring. Eleven years old, a little older than my daughter, with light brown skin and brown curls flying out behind her. There were other children trying to stand on their horses, but none was so accomplished as this granddaughter. She turned upside down and stood on her head.

It was thirty years ago I knew Mia, the grandmother, and we were not so careful about what we said thirty years ago; Mia had three bambini, all with a German father, and we used to say they were not black or white, they were gray. They were green, we said. We called them *les petits verts*. But you see—the eldest of *les petits verts* grew up to be a film actress like her mother, and had this daughter who can stand on her head on a horse in the Polo Club in Paris. The little girl came from the horses and kissed me hello, on the left and right, with a shining face and blue eyes. Life is long, when you live a long time—that seems a simple fact, but you don't know it until you have a lunch like this one.

Mia's husband—my dear friend, my brother—was called Renard. I played guitar then, and I was young. You have to be young to play the guitar, unless you are very great. It took me ten years to discover I had no ear, and five years more to discover I had no head to remember the words. My fingers, my technique, they were above the rest, but I was not gifted. Renard was gifted. He played the piano more beautifully than you have ever heard, with no music, all by ear. He could play anything. He used to help me, writing down the music, working out the harmonies, teaching me songs. We played at parties—not for money, because that was not our aim, but people asked us to come, and we had a trumpet and bass and clarinet and the whole thing.

Renard had some money, and he was raised with a rich life. Because of the music, he met a girl, Elsa, who was a little blonde *operettiche* singer, with a little voice. Elsa had a daughter, and she and the child were always with Renard. After some years, Renard said, "I have to marry this girl. I can't *not* marry this girl." We all said, Why? Keep on like you are. But he had to marry her, for his soul maybe, I don't know. He adopted the child and I became godfather, and then Elsa became jealous of Renard's ability, of his success and his friends, and she started to drink.

At this time I married my first wife, and I could not impose Renard and his family on my wife. I loved Renard, and the child was my goddaughter, but Elsa was too much. When this happens, you grow apart, and I did not see him for some years. Eventually he divorced her.

We were close again, when he divorced, and we had the same friends at the Travellers' Club and in the south. When he met Mia, the actress from Martinique, we all understood. She was so sexy, and he loved her, and she was fun. But she had the not-black, not-white bambini from the German, and this was Paris, and Paris was not so generous. It was not so well accepted then, to have these children. They all moved south to a big white house in Cap-Ferrat, and Renard had some money still, but he was gambling it away. My wife would not go to visit there, but I went. It was like a colony. The girl Mia and the green bambini were only the beginning. There were also the girl's two sisters, with bambini of their own. Kids all over the house, you did not know whose. They always had guests, because they had poker games in the house, and the guests came to take Renard's money. When he was out of money he would sit at the piano, and they shouted out what to play.

Finally Renard said he was going to marry the girl Mia. Just like the first time, with Elsa, he said he couldn't *not* marry her. We didn't understand, but we went to the wedding, and drove in a parade down to the sea at Cap-Ferrat. Everyone felt a little embarrassed, with the family not approving, and all the father-less bambini in wedding clothes, and the drunken blonde first wife in the memory. But Renard acted very happy, and flew his new wife and his friends to Miami, to go on a yacht to Martinique. I didn't go on the yacht, of course, but some did.

They went to La Dominique, with the moving sands. There is a big sign there that says, DANGEROUS BEACH. The water is very shallow and the sand is loose and deep, like quicksand. It sucks you down into the water, and the currents pull you out into the sea. The laughing girl, home again, swung her legs on the deck of the boat. The beach is not authorized, but Renard went swimming. With his debts and his adopted children and his family and his gambling, he went in at the unauthorized beach. He was a strong swimmer, but a strong swimmer is not what you need at La Dominique.

What you need is to stop fighting, let the arms and legs go limp. If you let go, and don't fight, the sand sucks you down, but then the water takes you back to the surface. Spits you out. If you fight and try to swim, you die. They didn't find Renard's body. His friends on the boat looked a long time. I went to the beach myself when I heard, and walked up and down, as close to the water as possible without slipping into the sand. I stayed there two days, looking at the water and thinking about my friend, then I flew back to Paris, where I was getting a divorce and had a job. They found a jawbone a month later—the drowned body all eaten by sharks or whatever was there.

Mia and I did not talk of Renard's death when I saw her last week at the Polo, old but still the same, but we were both thinking of it. It was why she did not laugh so much, I know. She might have laughed more with another, but I brought the memory of Renard to her. It was not the thing to talk about. When I left the club, Mia said to me, "My life has been a good life, and Renard would be happy with that."

I had nowhere to be at that moment, so I walked back along the rue de Babylone, where I lived when I was young. I used to walk to work from there, and brought girls home to the apartment with the purple bathtub sunk low into the tile. Each job and each girl, at that time, was the most important thing in the world, and demanded everything. I was still young enough to play guitar not so well.

My second wife is young, the age of my first son, who played guitar too long and has made nothing of his life. She is beautiful, and sparkles like jewels when she is wearing none: skin like gold, white teeth and clear blue eyes. We have two small children. The more I see other children, the more I think

mine are the most attractive. Since I realized I was too old for
guitar and married, I have had two good lives, with two good
wives. I am a lucky man. When I ride in the country, not in circles but moving forward, all alone, I think what could happen,
to leave behind a widow. Nothing much would have to happen; my brother is younger than I, and already dead. But
sometimes I think I will fall from the horse, hit my head or
break my spine, with no one to help. I would leave the widow
that much sooner, and she would marry again and have two
lives, too, with two husbands. She is young enough for that,
the way she shines. And then sometimes I think I can outlive
them all.

When I reached home, and walked into the courtyard below
our apartment, I could hear my son screaming at his sister from
the windows above. The elevator is tiny and slow, and when
the children race it on the stairs, they win. I took the stairs, too,
many at a time, and reached the third floor with my heart in
my ears and a dizziness across my eyes. I opened the apartment
door and climbed the last steps past the umbrellas. The keys
fell from my hand at the top. My son Gaétan looked up and
slid to a halt in his socks, surprised to see me standing there.
Gaétan is seven, the age of reason, the age of charm.

"What is going on here?" I demanded, waiting for the dizzy
feeling to go. "What is the purpose of this noise that shakes the
building?"

His sister Alix ran out from her room, and there came an
absolute chaos, both arguing at once, and the dog barking.
Tati the Filipina came from the kitchen and started, too. Three

voices, like angry bells, plus the dog. *"Aqua Boulevard . . . Gaé-tan ne veut pas . . . Oliver . . . la merde . . . Maman . . . comme les autres—"*

"Stop!" I said.

I could see straight now, and I made them go slow. Gaétan first, then his sister, then Tati. To have some order. A child was giving a birthday party at Aqua Boulevard, with the waterslides and the pool that makes waves like an ocean. Alix wanted to go. Gaétan said the brother of the girl with the birthday was a jerk. They know this American word. *C'est un* jerk. My wife was not home, and Tati is only one person, so Alix could not go to the party without Gaétan. Oliver, my wife's dog, the dog she bought to make the children fight not so much, had done a shit on the rug. Tati had been all afternoon cleaning it up.

Gaétan is impatient. I started with him. I bent down on my stiff knees so he could see my eyes. "This is a lesson for you," I said. "You don't play with the jerk. There are other children. It's easy, yes?"

Gaétan frowned.

"Alix, you get your bathing suit," I said. She went wild, kissing me, hugging me, then she ran to her room. Gaétan made a terrible noise.

I said, "Tati, you want to go to Aqua Boulevard?"

Tati smiled. She was tired of dog shit, and she could sit with the other nannies by the pool with the waves.

"Gaétan," I said, taking his shoulders in my hands, "you go on the biggest waterslide, without your sister. I want to hear you did that today."

Sometimes my son has a face like a storm, and then it clears, and again he is the most attractive child I have ever seen.

He ran to his bedroom for his bathing suit. I gave Tati the money for a birthday present for the sister of the jerk.

"I'm going to take Oliver for a walk," I said. "I will teach him discipline."

Tati gave me the leash, a long orange strap, and the children kissed Oliver good-bye and went out the door. I had told my wife I was going to order a leather leash from Hermès, and it was a joke, but maybe I would. With Oliver's initials. Oliver danced at my feet, his toenails scraping on the wood floor. On the rug was a white towel where Tati had cleaned.

My wife studied for the dog like when you buy a house, and finally she bought a border terrier, a small dog, but not as small as the ridiculous dogs you see in the streets of Paris. Small enough for an apartment but not a dog to make you a fool. Oliver and I went down the elevator, out through the courtyard and toward the Luxembourg. He ran ahead of me on the orange strap. He was excited about everything, still a puppy. He didn't know not to sniff at women's shoes, like he didn't know not to shit on the carpet. I smiled at the women in the shoes and they smiled back. I had not wanted a dog, but the children loved him. It was true they did not fight so much now. The day my wife brought him home, my daughter held the dog in her arms and said, "This is the happiest day of my life." Children are whores. They will say anything. But I thought it could be true.

I had never trained a dog. I had not even taken this dog for a walk, because I could not take him for lunch at the Polo. When I was still working for the Greeks, with the shipping, we were given a beautiful Arabian horse, a king's horse. We had no use for it, but to slaughter it would offend the king, so it must be kept like a king's horse, and that was left to me. I found a stable, and thought I would ride in the Bois de Boulogne, but the horse would not cross the road. We reached the road each time, and then it stopped. The most elegant horse you have ever seen, afraid of roads. I tried a long time to make the horse cross, and then paid an old cavalry officer to train the horse in the cavalry style. Make the horse obey. Be the commander. He came back to me in six weeks and said the horse did not want to cross the road. So maybe Oliver did not want to shit outside. This would be a problem. We were at the street corner, almost to the *jardin,* and I was thinking how the dog would like to see the trees and the grass, and then Oliver ran on his long orange strap into the road. A Mercedes taxi hit him square with the tire.

Oliver did not move. There was no blood. I held him against my shirt and I could feel his small breaths. His eyes were half open but looked at nothing. The taxi was gone, and no one for me to shout at. I stood on the corner looking at the Jardin du Luxembourg across the street with its green grass, then turned to look at the shops, trying to think where was an animal doctor. I thought of going back to the Polo, where they would have a horse doctor. The beautiful Mia could still be there, and she knew death and would know what to do. But it was a foolish thought, and I began to walk down the street, looking at the names on the buildings for a doctor. The orange strap hit my ankles at each step. Then I remembered taxis as a help and I waved to one, holding the dog tightly in one arm. The taxi stopped, but by the time I was in, the breathing and the heartbeat were gone.

I let the taxi drive me home, though it was a short way,

because I didn't think I could stand to walk. In the car my thoughts were mixed up between the dog, and the taxi's tire, and Mia swinging her legs, and my friend drowning under the waves, and then I felt my lungs like ice and told the driver to take me to Aqua Boulevard. I had to see my children in front of me. I had sent them with only Tati to that ridiculous pool.

The taxi let me out at Aqua Boulevard with the dog in my arms. They would not let me take a dead dog, but I walked past the security smiling, holding Oliver's head up. Women carry their dogs in their arms all the time, and the gendarme looked at my face strangely, but said nothing. Past the security there is a glass wall to watch the slides and the pool, and I stood there with the dog. The room is enormous, full of people in bathing suits, fat ones and thin ones, all colors but all greenish through the water-spotted window, with the plastic tubes snaking around overhead and a glass roof to let in the sun. The horn blew that says the waves will start, and all the people ran into the water. I looked for my children but didn't see them there. I wanted to run in and find them, but I had no bathing suit and could not let them see their dog.

The waves rolled in to the concrete beach painted the color of sand. Small children rode the water to the shore, and there among the heads was Gaétan. My son's face, wide-eyed and afraid. The water pushed him to where he could touch the bottom and he stood, laughing. He raised his fists in the air and shouted, like a man who wins a boxing match, tired and happy. He ran back into the waves. I breathed again. There was still the feeling in my lungs, stopping the air to my chest, but it was melting.

The dog had grown stiff in my arms. I looked for my

daughter and saw her run across the painted beach into the water, her young body in a black bathing suit shining with wet. I leaned my head against the green glass, the warm dog still against my chest. I said thank you for my children and listened to the rushing of the waves that did not stop but came and came again.

THE RIVER

SOMETHING IS WRONG with Jo and I don't know what it is.

I wake in the screenhouse to the sound of Mack trucks going seventy down the road outside the fence. The trucks carry uranium tailings from the Superfund site in the valley north of us. It's Saturday and I'm home from the Forest Service, and Jo's home, too. I turn over slowly in my sleeping bag, trying not to disturb her with my rustling, and find her tucked in with her head on her pillow, looking at me.

"Been awake long?" I ask her.

"No," she says. "Just now." She smiles like she always does in the morning when she really wakes up, after her open-eyed but unrecognizing first moments. Morning is the only time Jo's smiles seem unsolicited; the rest of the time she's so quiet and serious that when something makes her smile, even she looks surprised.

She turns to see if Inger is awake: our houseguest on the screenhouse floor. She's not, so Jo settles back in, her hair sticking in staticky strands to the nylon sleeping bag. Her skin is too yellow, except around her eyes, where it's too white. She's thinner than she used to be, without trying; at thirty-two she has the body of a girl. All the hair on her arms and legs has disappeared. She claims the wind blew it off while she was watching birds, but she's dry inside and out. I frown at her and she knows what I'm thinking.

"Fitz, I'm fine," she says. "It's the wind and the heat."

During the week Jo sits in a clearing outside La Sal for eight hours every day in hundred-and-five-degree temperatures. The wind has been at least forty knots every day, sometimes fifty and sixty, and it hasn't rained all summer. She baby-sits peregrine falcons and breeding bald eagles, and her lashless eyes are white-circled from whole days peering through binoculars, waiting for fledglings to emerge from aeries. Her eagles have kept a spare nest all summer, a nest they don't seem to use, like it's there for emergencies. So she has three nests to monitor, one empty, two full, and she never looks up from her lenses. I play with the soft down on her cheek and note that it's still there. It's under her arms, too, and she says it'll grow back on her arms and legs.

I slide out of bed, find my shoes and step over Inger in her sleeping bag by the door. Her guitar leans against the screen wall and I'm careful not to bump it. She opens her eyes and smiles at me when I ease the door closed.

The Forest Service let me salvage the screenhouse to live in until we build. It's twelve feet by twelve, with a solid roof, and it held pamphlets on wildlife on the Colorado River before I reassembled it here. We have to bring water in, so I hike to the well, swinging the empty six-gallon bottle against the tamarisk, and thinking what to do about the knapweed. The well is a good, deep one, and the water comes up clear. From the pump I can see the bluffs across the river a half mile away, but mostly I can see sky. After a week down in a canyon, I can never wait to get back to a full-sized sky, to weather I can see coming.

I lug the heavy bottle back, and the women are sitting up, with their legs swaddled in their sleeping bags like puffy blue mermaids. From outside the screenhouse they look like twins, in their braids. They've been best friends since college, since before I knew Jo. I can hear their voices from outside, deep alto voices that make strangers think they're tired, but I can't hear what they're saying. When I come into the screenhouse they stop talking, and smile up at me. I'm forty-nine, so much older than both of them, and still they flummox me.

"What?" I say.

They just smile. Up close, Jo has a knowing look, a canniness that Inger lacks. But Inger doesn't need to be knowing, as far as I can tell. A Minnesota heiress with dairymaid braids and a lineless tan, she's like something you'd make up, and she treats the world like something she made up. We hear from her only when she'll be in Utah or when she wants us to go with her somewhere else. She stretches her arms over her head, in a man's white undershirt. Jo thinks there's something permanently unfinished about Inger—like the missing "id" of her name, though I guess it's not an id that's missing—and that's why she's never with a man very long; there's an absence in her that doesn't seem to need filling, or that other people can't fill.

"Inger's going to pull burdock with you," Jo says. "I have to write up my bird reports."

"I want to," Inger says, before I can say she doesn't have to.

They both climb out of their sleeping bags, and I watch the top of Jo's head while she rummages in a dry box. Her hair has dulled, and her shoulders look thin. She digs out canvas work gloves for Inger, and I can tell movement costs her; she moves slow. When I described the changes to my father on the phone, he said it might be anemia and the climate, and to make sure she had iron and water.

Inger dresses and we pull burdock all morning, piling it to burn when it's dry. I want to ask her about Jo, about what they were saying, but I don't. The work is hypnotic: grab the plant low, yank it out, shake soil off the roots, throw it on the pile. It's hard to measure time when the sun feels like it's not moving, shining hot on your back.

"Jo loves you," Inger says, right next to me, out of the blue.

I hadn't realized she was so close. Her T-shirt is off, tucked into the back of her shorts, and she struggles with a waist-high plant until it comes out at the root, sending her a few steps backward. She tosses the weed on the pile. Her chest and throat are shiny with beads of sweat, dark against her white bra. I give her my water bottle and she lifts her braids to pour it over the back of her neck and her throat, the white sticking to her breasts in pink rivulets where the water runs down.

At noon we eat sandwiches inside and I try to decide what to do with the tamarisk that has grown up around the cotton-woods. It's an imported species and it's everywhere, indestructible. Cutting it down won't kill it, and poison might kill the birds, but if I leave it, it will choke out the cottonwoods. More Superfund trucks thunder by with their radioactive loads, wearing down the southbound side of a road not designed to carry that much weight.

The sun drops a little from directly overhead, and the clouds cast small, round shadows on the bluffs across the river. Jo gives Inger a wide-brimmed straw hat to keep the sun off her face, and the two of them climb ahead of me over the neighbor's fence to the field where he's keeping a few cows and horses out for the summer. The dry burdock and the goatheads stick to our shoes, so we look for high ground and walk on the bare, uneven ridges left by the plow. Jo's straw-colored braid swings between her shoulder blades. She wears sandals and a white cotton dress she's had since we met. Her arms are bare and the definition is gone beneath the smooth, too-yellow skin. Her freckles look lighter.

I always thought Jo would grow out of me. She didn't have a dad and I thought I was the replacement dad, and one day she would leave home. Or she'd decide she wanted kids and a guy who could pay for them. Or I thought I'd do something stupid on the river and she would be a young widow who gets to have another twenty or thirty years with someone else. I used to think who it might be: a doctor like my dad, a divorced guy with kids, one of our friends living in a converted garage in Telluride. But I didn't plan for a second life without her.

We reach the cottonwoods along the river, and the bare spots between the trees are fine white sand like the well diggers dug up beneath the red dust and the knapweed. The summer drought has left the river running low, the color of coffee with milk, and shallow all the way across the channel. I take off my cap and my shorts. Jo pulls her dress over her head and tugs it free of her braid, and she is naked underneath. She hangs the dress on a young tamarisk and steps barefoot down the bank, up to her knees in the brown water, and then she turns to look at me and smiles. Her breasts are the same, the one thing about her body that hasn't changed.

"It's nice," she says. "It's cold." She walks out into the river. The color of her skin is pale and even across her ass and down the backs of her legs, with a shadow of tan in the small of her back and on her shoulders.

It is cold, but the cold feels good. Inger slips off her tank top and shorts and leaves them on top of the straw hat. Then she's thigh-deep in the river and God is she lovely, dragging her hands across the surface at her sides. For a flat river at low water it moves fast, opening puddles around each of her fingers.

At the deepest part of the channel I hear a shriek, and above us are two peregrines, one on either side of the river, hunting together. They both stop in trees and stare down at us, black-masked and hunched in the shoulders. The one on the right gives a high-pitched *kek kek kek*.

"That's an immature," Jo says, sculling with her hands against the current. "The other one is teaching it to hunt."

"Call to them," I say.

Jo digs in her heels and shakes water off her hands. When she cups them to her mouth and whistles, the younger bird stops his screeching and looks down. The parent ignores Jo, dives on a near vertical to the surface of the river, and flies south with what looks like a merganser in its talons. The younger bird, with a last look at Jo, leaves his tree and follows the burdened adult, catching up, circling back, screeching to be fed. They disappear downriver.

"I got my show for today," Jo says. "I'm going back." She ducks under the swirling brown current one last time, and comes up blinking while water streams from her face and hair. She wades for shore, like something from a dream. "Stay and swim," she says, "I'll save you shower water." She slips her dress over her head. There's a long silence while we watch her go.

"Can you get her to go to a doctor?" I ask Inger.

"No one's ever gotten Jo to do anything," Inger says.

"Now's the time."

"I've told her that. She doesn't want to go."

"I'd pay for it."

"I would, too," Inger says. "She says no."

I watch downriver where the birds went and something sinks in me, some chance I thought I had. I grab for the remaining one. "My father's coming," I say. "I've asked him to. He'll look at her."

"She needs blood tests. Your dad can't do blood tests in the screenhouse."

I look at Inger again. Her face is hard, but then it crumples. Fear for Jo has become more familiar to me than my own hands, more expected than the every-five-minutes trucks on the highway, but now it blazes up again, so I can hardly see through it. Inger's close enough to touch, and I wipe her cheek with my thumb.

"That's supposed to help?" I ask.

She laughs and moves toward me. I can feel the outline of her face against my chest, the hollow of her eyes, the curve of her nose. I'm naked under the water and nervous to have her so close. I squeeze her narrow shoulders with both arms and tell her Jo'll be okay. *Is* okay. Inger eases herself away from me, then splashes water on her face, so her eyelashes stick together in spiky points. We dress on the bank without looking at each other, then she stands on her toes to kiss my mouth. She's kissed me before, as a joke, in Jo's presence, but I've never noticed the wetness inside her lower lip or the pressure of her hand on my arm as she reaches up to me.

We walk back through the pasture, and when we reach the screenhouse, Jo sits naked on a cooler, combing her hair in long even strands. When she sees us, she ducks inside. The solar-shower bag hangs on the boat rack on the truck, and Inger goes first. I sit on the truck's bumper with my back to her and look at my hands on my knees: rough old boatman's hands that Jo complains are scratchy. The thumb that touched Inger's cheek is cracked and dry.

Inger finishes her shower, wrapped in her towel. She smells like strawberries. A reddish station wagon drives by on the road, too far away to see us. Inger takes my place on the truck's bumper and asks if I ever wanted kids.

The water is almost too hot from the day's sun and I let it run over my face before I answer her. I shrug, but she can't see me, so I say, "Not really." If I had a kid, I'd want to give it too many things I can't provide. A good school, a permanent home, a childhood on a lake.

Jo comes from the house in jeans, carrying necklaces of plastic flowers in rainbow colors. "Look what I found!" she says. She hangs one lei around Inger's neck and one around mine. She kisses my cheek. "Now you look festive," she says.

"King and Queen Kalikimaka. I'm going to town for ice and phone calls."

At the gate, still in my towel, I lean in the window of the truck to ask if she's feeling all right, if she's drinking enough water.

"Thanks, doc," Jo says, and she shakes her head at me. "You sound like your dad." Then she pulls down the road, out into the slipstream of an eighteen-wheeler.

Inger carries a lawn chair and her guitar into the tamarisk to even her tan. I stay at the house, fixing the door, setting a tiny lizard free outside, deciding whether to fill the gaps where the corrugated roof meets the walls, trying not to think about Jo's sickness or Inger's nakedness in the tamarisk. In the cotton-woods, a meadowlark sings a repeated series of double notes.

Jo returns with the ice and a grocery bag of apricots from the man with the backhoe. "Where's Inger?" she asks.

"Sunbathing," I say, my mouth dry.

"Take her some apricots," Jo says, placing three in my hand.

Inger sits, as I expected, naked in the lawn chair by the dry streambed. She's picking out chords, and when she sees me, she hugs the guitar to her chest and brings her knees up, smiling.

"Apricots," I say, and put them in her outstretched hand. "You look lovely."

She gives me a conspiratorial look, and I leave quickly. Inside the house, Jo rubs a cream that smells like cucumbers on her paper-smooth skin.

"I don't like to be without you," I tell her.

"We needed ice," Jo says. "We can't leave Inger alone with the coyotes." She drops the jar of cream into a drawstring bag.

"I mean I don't ever like to be without you," I say.

Jo's smile starts around her mouth, tentative, like I've caught her off-guard, then lifts her whole face and her fragile-looking eyes into an unexpected coughed laugh. "Since when?" she says. "We're apart all the time, we've been apart all our lives." She puts half an apricot in my mouth and tells me they're good for me, I need to keep up my strength.

The moon is taking its time tonight. Inger gets out her guitar and sings, and her voice is sweet and clear, like water. She sings "Bobby McGee," and "Many Rivers to Cross," and "Summertime" and the one that goes, "I wish I had a river, I could skate away on." She closes her eyes when the words are about sex, like she's embarrassed and can't keep her voice strong if she looks at us. I lie on my back on my sleeping bag and Jo falls asleep beside me. The room is bright with the full moon when Inger puts away the guitar.

"Jo's asleep," she says.

Quiet settles into the screenhouse. Inger crosses her arms over her knees and buries her nose in the crook of her elbow, eyes wide-open and watching the wall. Suddenly I don't want to be in the screenhouse with her; I push away my sleeping bag and pick up my shoes.

"Going for a walk," I say.

I walk through the tamarisk to the fence, the echoes of Inger's voice playing over the memory of the two women in the silty river, the water pushing us downstream. Inger's eyes closing when she sang, "Loved me so naughty made me weak in the knees." A breeze is blowing, warm and from the west, and the moon is big on the horizon over the bluffs. I think of Jo in the water, holding on against the current as sand slipped away downriver, bound for the Pacific. I know Jo wants for me what she thinks I would want for her, but I imagined a second life for her only because I didn't believe in it. I never believed I could give her up.

When I return, Inger leans in the door of the screenhouse watching me, knee cocked, and I wonder where her calm comes from.

"You have to walk out there, just to the fence," I tell her.

"Come with me," Inger says.

I have to clear my throat to speak again. "You should go alone."

Inger smiles to herself and pulls on her sandals. I watch her walk to the fence, the wind blowing her skirt between her legs until she pushes it away and it billows off to the side. She leans on the fence and looks up at the moon for a long while. Finally she walks back through the weeds and puts her arms around me where I'm still standing in the door. She rests her head against my chest again and I can feel my heart beating against her cheek.

"Jo'll be all right," she says.

"She will," I say.

Inger nods, not looking up. She stays with me a minute longer, then moves past me into the screenhouse to bed.

At 4 A.M. I wake and not a single truck goes by on the highway. I wait in the silence while my eyes adjust, and Jo turns over in her unzipped bag and sighs, eyes closed. I brush her hair from her face and she mumbles something I can't understand. Then she raises herself on her elbow with a gasp and looks toward the river. "Inger!" she calls out softly. "Inger!" She clutches my arm and her eyes are wide.

"She's here," I say. "She's asleep."

"Oh," she says, looking around the room. Her breathing slows. "I thought the water was rising," she says. "I thought Inger was out in the river and I wasn't watching." She turns to look at the sleeping bag by the door, Inger's braid snaking out of it in the moonlight, and she says, "It's all right. It's okay." She slides back down into bed, still mostly asleep. I stroke her dried and drying hair until she turns away from me.

I watch, listening to the slow breathing in the room, until the moon has sunk below the bluffs. To put myself to sleep I try to remember every object in my father's examining room when I was a kid. The stethoscope, the small sink, the high white bed, the jars of cotton. The framed certificates he didn't notice any more than he noticed the doors or the windows, but that made him seem able to help people. I used to read the embossed words, the important signatures, my father's name, thinking what he did was good, and I would try to do the same.

KITE WHISTLER
AQUAMARINE

WINTER WAS BAD when it was just ordinary cold and dark and a smoky haze hung over town because everyone had woodstoves blazing in spite of the burning restrictions. Then the temperature dropped overnight to twenty below, and a Thoroughbred filly was born at our house, early, before we expected her.

I was still in bed when my husband found her because I had been awake until four, thinking about why I couldn't sleep. I didn't hear Cort go out to feed the horses, but I heard him struggling with the screen door, and when I came downstairs he had set the foal down on a tarp laid out on the carpet. She was chestnut like her mother, and had thin white arcs of frostbite on the tips of her ears. Cort had wrapped her in a blanket and sat with her on the floor.

"She's so early," I said.

"I didn't have the mare in the foaling shed." His glasses were fogged and he ran a hand under his nose. I gave him a tissue from the box in the kitchen.

"Can you keep her on the tarp? Off the carpet?" I asked.

He looked at me.

"I'm sorry," I said.

He pulled the shivering foal closer to his body. He'd been banking on this horse. The stud belonged to a client, and had Derby bloodlines. Cort had traded attorney's fees for stud fees because he didn't have the stud fees in the bank, which drove me a little crazy. He'd won a case that winter for more money than either of us had ever made, and every penny went to pay off his horse debts. Breeding the mare had meant committing to the horse business, which wasn't a real business at all.

"Have you called the vet?" I asked. The foal wasn't struggling or trying to stand up. She curled into Cort's lap like a long-legged cat.

"I can't reach him," Cort said. "I can't tell how long she's been out there." The foal's hair was damp and fine. "I have to get milk for her," he said. "Will you hold her a minute?"

"Oh, Cort," I said. If I avoided touching animals I could pretend I was part of the free-breathing world, one of the happy millions who hugged dogs and slept with cats and lay their cheeks against the smooth throats of horses. But my lungs wouldn't take it; they shut down. We kept all horse clothes out of the house, and I'd made, across the lawn from Cort's stables, a world apart from dander and hair.

"The blanket's clean," he said. "Just hold it around her for a minute. I'll be right back." He eased the filly off his lap. I held the blanket to her tiny body with both hands, careful not to let her touch my sleeves. Sleeves caught dander, brushed against my face, went inside other sleeves. Cort let the screen door swing shut behind him, and the filly started. Her eyes were glassy and unfocused. I waited, bent over, and the foal held very still. I could feel her breathing. My legs began to ache, and my nose to itch. I had a client getting out of prison and I was due to pick her up that morning, ninety miles away.

Cort came back with white spots from the cold on his cheeks and a bowl of thick gray liquid in his bare hands.

"The antibodies in the first milk don't last long," he said. "It's still too cold out there for her to nurse." He grabbed a clean tea towel, soaked the twisted end of the cloth in the bowl and held it to the foal's lips until she sucked at it halfheartedly. "Is there anything like a bottle here?" he asked.

I opened a cupboard: a wide-mouthed thermos. Tupperware. Measuring cups.

"This'll work," Cort said, dipping the cloth again in the sticky gray milk.

I washed my hands to the elbows and drove to the women's prison in Billings. Cort stayed home with the foal.

Ruth Finson was my only criminal client, and she was getting out on appeal. I was meeting her with the county people and her six-year-old daughter. Ruth had been convicted of narcotics manufacture in Montana two years earlier, and it had taken that long to convince the judge that the racket was her husband's business, not hers—mostly because that wasn't exactly true. During that time Ruth's daughter had been growing up in foster care and starting school. Cort helped me with the case when the foster parents sued for custody, and we won. We made an odd team: Cort took everything to trial, and wrote briefs the night before they were due. He counted on other people's laziness, their underestimation of him, their inability to handle their own disorganization as well as he handled his. I planned ahead, negotiated everything, hedged bets. I might not have taken the custody battle on my own, but by the time we went before the judge, I'd had enough of the foster parents' self-righteousness and was grateful to Cort for his help.

I drove to Billings vowing to cut him more slack about his horses and to take more pro bono cases. Two self-improvement projects. But I knew they wouldn't last. I couldn't love the horses when they had my house in hock, and I needed all the working time I had.

It was the little girl's sixth birthday, and I stopped at Safeway for a pink-frosted cake in case no one else had done anything. I guessed the foster parents would leave the celebration to the mother, and I knew Ruth couldn't have made any preparations. When I got to the prison, the little girl was already waiting with a social worker. The foster parents hadn't come, but they had dressed her in a way that suggested ownership: she wore a short, pleated turquoise skirt over turquoise tights and bright pink shoes. Someone had buttoned her pink sweater at the throat and put her hair in two pigtails that curled. She looked small and uncertain, and she came to sit by me in the orange plastic chairs in the waiting room. I didn't know if she remembered me. The social worker watched us.

"Hi, kiddo," I said.

The little girl grinned shyly. "You called me kiddo," she said.

"Don't you like that name?"

She considered. "It's okay. My real name is Lauren." The adult name from my files sounded old in her small voice.

"Lauren, then."

She nodded, and swung her pink shoes in an arc above the spotted gray linoleum. For two years she had seen her mother only with a warden's supervision, every week at first, until the long drive became a hassle to the overworked social worker and the visits became more intermittent. There were no grandparents to take her, and her father was serving a twenty-year sentence. Two uncles and an aunt were also in prison, and another aunt had left the state and refused custody of Lauren. So Lauren had spent two birthdays in foster care.

"This is a big day," I said. "Not everybody turns six and gets to see their mom on the same day."

"Did you know it was my birthday?" she asked.

"I did," I said, and waited for an account of any celebrations. "Have you had a party yet?" I ventured.

"We had pony rides and a duck piñata with candy inside," she said. "The pony was my favorite."

For a moment it seemed better that Ruth stay in prison than come out and hear about pony rides with foster parents.

I said, "My husband has baby horses, sort of like ponies. You can't ride them, but you could bring your mom to see them if you want." I thought of Cort on the floor with the foal.

"Do you ride the momma horses?" Lauren asked.

"They make me sneeze," I said. "But I'll ask my husband if you can ride them."

The social worker stood across the waiting room. She had recommended the foster parents for custody, impressed with their big house and their solidity, and now she acted like she'd been voted out. No other relatives or friends showed up. When Ruth finally came out in her court clothes, she knelt and took her daughter in her arms. Lauren stood straight in her bright sweater, patting her mother on the back. The social worker left by herself, and I went out to my car to put the birthday cake in the trunk. I didn't know how to present it. It seemed meager next to the piñata party, and cruel to call attention to Ruth's empty-handedness.

Lauren had her seat belt on before I got the key in the ignition. Ruth slipped into the passenger seat and stared out the window as we drove. Her hands looked thin in her lap. I asked careful questions of them both until Lauren began a tentative monologue about kindergarten.

When I got home in the afternoon, the horse was gone from the kitchen and the house was cold. There was a plastic baby bottle on the kitchen counter. The kitchen doors were both closed, so I went through to the greenhouse, where the sliding-glass door was open and the ferns were freezing. I was sliding the heavy door shut when I saw Cort in the hot tub on the deck, naked to the waist, with the new foal slick and wet on his lap, his arm over her neck to hold her down in the hot water. I stepped outside into the sharper cold.

"Throw me that towel," Cort said. "I need to keep her ears warm."

I handed him the towel, making a mental note not to use it

myself—it was striped and blue—and he wrapped it around the foal's head so her forelock tufted out from the terry cloth. She lifted her nose in protest.

"I had to warm her up," he said. "She keeps shivering. The vet's in Great Falls."

I watched them for a while, each breath stabbing my lungs. "It's below zero every winter," I finally said.

He glared at me over fogged glasses and said nothing. Frost formed on the invisible hairs around the filly's velvet nose, bringing each hair into white-sheathed focus. My ears began to sting and I put my hands over them.

"Maybe you shouldn't raise horses here," I said, hearing my own voice muffled. "Or maybe we should move."

He ignored me and adjusted the filly's turban to keep the towel dry. Water from the tub froze in sheets of white on the planks of the deck. I went inside to warm up. The tarp was still on the floor in the room off the kitchen, and I felt my chest tighten. I counted the hours I had lain awake the night before, went upstairs, took off my shoes and climbed into bed. It was three o'clock. Kids would be getting out of school.

I woke up as the sun was going down, and put on a bathrobe. Cort sat on the floor with the foal, nursing it and keeping it warm. We ate leftover chicken and salad foraged from the fridge. I thought about bringing in the birthday cake from the trunk, but figured it was frozen solid, so I stood in my bathrobe at the woodstove until my legs stung, then went back upstairs. Cort stayed awake all night. I heard him get up a few times and walk around while I lay in bed, unable to sleep. He was still holding the foal, on the tarp on the floor, when I got up in the morning. I drove to work with itching eyes, telling myself it was only lack of sleep that was limiting my peripheral vision. The horse had only been in one room, after all.

The next week the cold spell broke, exposing the dead brown grass of winter lawns. A family of woodpeckers had made a home in the wood siding of my bedroom wall and the babies woke with the sun, demanding to be fed. I woke with them, aching for sleep. For a few days it was warm enough to go without a coat. Willows budded, duped by the early thaw. I threw away the ruined cake. The snow receded in the mountains.

Ruth called to ask if she could bring Lauren to see the horses, and I went out with Cort, staying upwind of the stables, while he caught and saddled a mare for Lauren to ride. The vet had come, and said the foal had frostbitten tendons. Her legs were wrapped up and sore, and she wasn't walking well; the frostbite had worn the hide on her hocks almost down to the bone. Her mother nosed and nickered at her to stand. Cort let them out of the heated stall, and we watched the foal step gingerly toward her mother, sit down to rest and struggle to her feet again to nurse when her mother came close.

"Will she be able to run?" I asked. She had the long, straight legs of a fast horse, but they folded suddenly beneath her. She had to be in pain.

"I don't know," he said.

"Is it worth it to keep her alive?"

"Is it *worth* it?" he said.

I waited for a real answer, but none came. Ruth pulled up the driveway in a blue Skylark with Lauren in the passenger seat, and we didn't have to finish the conversation. Lauren wore a puffy pink winter coat and flowered corduroy pants. She saw the shivering baby in the corral, and asked her name.

"She doesn't have one yet," Cort said. He was keeping the blank registration papers in a kitchen drawer with his keys and spare change. He didn't even call her "the filly," he called her "the baby." She seemed too invalid to be a horse, too fragile to support a proper name. "What do you think it should be?" he asked.

Lauren looked hard at the filly. "I don't know," she said. "She looks cold."

Cort picked up the filly and carried her back into the heated stall, followed by the anxious mare, and closed the gate.

"Are the horses making you sneeze?" Lauren asked me, looking up from the hood of her pink coat.

"I'm all right," I said. "I just can't touch them or get too close."

Lauren frowned, and then she nodded. Cort lifted her left foot into the shortened stirrup, and helped her swing her body over the saddled mare. He gave her the reins and led her into the field.

Ruth leaned against the chewed-up wooden fence, watching her daughter ride away. She looked healthier already, and she moved and talked more easily. Her dark blonde hair was tied in a loose knot at the nape of her neck. She told me she didn't want to get too settled in her new apartment because she'd be leaving soon. She was moving in with a man she knew, in a cabin forty miles from town.

"How will Lauren get to school?" I asked.

"We'll drive her," Ruth said.

"That road is bad in winter."

"He has a truck," Ruth said. "I don't know. Maybe I'll home-school."

"You need state approval for that," I said.

"Yeah."

"Will you have running water?"

"There's a well," she said. "Marvin is very close to nature. He has a teepee set up out there in the summer."

I nodded, and looked out at Cort and Lauren on the far side of the field. Lauren held the reins high in her puffy coat. Cort nodded at whatever she was saying.

"Does Marvin have a job?" I asked Ruth.

"He's a holistic healer," she said. "He's not working right now. He hunts."

"What's in season?" I asked.

She shrugged one shoulder and pushed a wisp of hair away from her cheek with one thin hand. Her voice had a defiant edge. "Only what we need."

Cort brought Lauren past the stables again, and the girl reached down to stroke the mare's neck, talking to it; the mare turned back her ears to listen.

"Time to go," Ruth called.

Lauren looked reluctant, then said, "Okay." Cort helped her down and showed her how to tie the lead rope to the fence.

"The baby should be called Kite Whistler Aquamarine," Lauren said.

Cort said it was a fine name and it would stick. Ruth held the passenger door for her daughter, then drove off down the dirt road without saying good-bye. Cort unsaddled the mare and brushed her. I moved to stay upwind.

"Ruth's taking Lauren to live with a mountain man in the woods," I told him. "A poacher who lives in a teepee."

Cort pulled a handful of hair out of the brush and let it fall to the ground, where it blew across the clumps of manure and dirt. "Do you think the foster parents still want her?" he asked.

"I don't know," I said. "I don't think they should have her either."

Cort dumped a coffee can full of oats into a bucket and carried the saddle into the tack room. "I don't know what to tell you," he said. "Not much you can do about other people's kids."

"Ruth thinks she's going to home-school her," I said.

"*That* you might be able to do something about," he said. "Maybe. Probably be pro bono." He gave me half a grin.

I stayed while he checked on the filly. He tried to get her to nurse, but she couldn't stand, so he picked her up, supporting her on his thighs, until she got a purchase and sucked hungrily. When she let go of the teat, he took off the bandages on her ankles, and the bare tendons were red and inflamed beneath.

Cort rewrapped the ankles with antibiotic salve, and set the baby on clean blankets to keep her out of the dirt and straw. The mare licked at the bandages, nudging the foal to stand. When we went inside, Cort took off his horsey jacket at the door.

That evening and all the next day, Cort went out to the field every three hours to pick up the filly and let her nurse. I went to work and to the law library, and called a few teachers to find out how the rules about home-schooling were enforced. When

I came back, Cort's truck was in the driveway, but the house was empty. I dropped the mail on the counter, and he came in through the side door, wearing his jacket.

"The jacket," I said.

He took it off and left it on the bench outside.

"You were right about what people get away with," I said. "There might as well not be any home-schooling regulations."

Cort washed his hands a long time, ran a glass of water from the tap and looked at the ceiling as he drank it. I flipped through the stack of envelopes. Nothing with friendly handwriting on it.

"I'm thinking Ruth will get tired of the idea," I said. "Or of the guy. But I might get her some schoolbooks in the meantime."

Cort set his water glass down by the sink. "The baby's feet are falling off," he said. "One of them's already gone."

"Oh, God."

"The tendon isn't growing back and there's nothing there to hold the feet on," he said. "Perfectly good horse except she's not going to have any feet." His voice cracked on the word "feet." He turned and rummaged through his kitchen drawer, beneath unpaid bills and Kite's registration papers, until he found two small keys on a ring that jangled in his hand. I watched him go into the laundry room, unlock the file cabinet there and bring out a pistol with a revolving chamber. The gun dangled awkwardly in his hand.

"That leg just ends in a bony point," he said. "The rest will go if she tries to stand up again. I have blankets over her so she can't get up. They can't cry, you know. She's just out there sweating in the cold."

He sat down at the table, and set the revolver in front of him with a click. It looked like a child's western toy. I thought of the mare nosing off Cort's blankets in a panic, trying to get to her baby.

"Does that thing work?" I asked.

"If you stand close enough." He turned it to point away. The chair creaked beneath his weight.

"Is there another way to put her down?"

"I wish she could die on her own," he said. "But she'd just be hurting."

I took his hand off the revolver, leaving the gun on the table. His skin was clean from tap water, chapped from lifting the baby outside without gloves. I raised the hand to my face to feel it rough and cold on my skin, and he moved to let me sit on his knee.

He made a noise that sounded like a sob but couldn't be; I'd never seen him cry. The baby was outside waiting, and Cort's hair against my face smelled like shampoo and hay. He put his arms around me and pulled me closer, and we sat there a long time, not saying anything, so the filly could stay.

LAST OF THE
WHITE SLAVES

We MOVED TO THE stone terrace after dinner, to coffees laid out on the low table. The men had resigned themselves to not being offered brandy; they would pirate the bottle when Eugénie went to bed. The wind was down and the sea flat all the way to the dark island of Poros, with its cluster of village lights; on the low table, a candle in a glass shield burned still and straight. I watched through the mounted telescope as the young Greek couple across the bay drew their blinds for the night. North in the Balkans, NATO was bombing, but here it was quiet.

"It's terrible," Eugénie said. "You don't know what it's like to be in a city with bombs coming down."

It was true, we didn't. There were five of us, all younger than

Eugénie. My husband and I, Americans, were counted the most ignorant and most at fault. The new arrivals were an English couple, too young to have known war. The extra man was French and even younger; he sat at Eugénie's side at dinner and flattered her. Eugénie claimed Greece, though her accent was British, and her passport could have been anything, with all her husbands.

"I don't know if I should stay here," she said. "The Turks will take Cyprus now, with everything in chaos."

No one answered. I think we didn't know which was less likely: an invasion, or Eugénie fleeing the Peloponnesus in her eighties, for any reason. Eugénie invited my husband to Greece every summer because she wanted him to publish her memoir. She had lived a remarkable life but didn't have a remarkable book, and it dragged through slow ghostwritten revisions. Every year, at work in the hot city, I thought of blue water and white bougainvillea and forgot how exhausting it was to be her guest, to stay in favor and say the right thing. So each summer we would arrive, look at the new draft, give careful suggestions that would not be taken, and find ourselves on the terrace waiting for her to trip mercifully off to bed.

"It's terrible," Eugénie said again.

The silence went on too long; Eugénie broke it.

"Miles Sheffield was here a week ago," she said. "He came alone."

Here there was interest. Here was news, not opinion, and we jumped at it. Eugénie drew her white wrap across her throat to keep off the breeze that wasn't there. Her eyes shone with the awareness of an audience; she had found her topic.

I had met Miles Sheffield at Eugénie's house years before.

He was English, and traveled with a young man named Christopher who seemed more like a child than a companion. Gregarious and impossible, Christopher demanded loud music at dinner and dropped arch hints to Eugénie's chef to make lemon meringue pie instead of the chocolate he hated. The week I met them, the chef served chocolate every night: a mousse, a cake, a soufflé, a layered torte, chocolate ice cream at lunch, working Christopher into a barely concealed rage. Christopher was blond and tan, and got by on his looks, but it was Miles who brought him along.

Miles was an asset to everyone; he made a living at it. He knew every name that came up at any dinner, and the stories he told made his listeners wish he would tell stories about them. He had left his legal studies to take a job with the British ambassador to Saudi Arabia, where he made himself indispensable. He was the ambassador's lover and his protégé, and he assimilated to Arab life faster than anyone since T. E. Lawrence. When the old ambassador died, Miles stayed on. When I asked what he did exactly (it was something for the embassy still, some diplomatic role), he said he was the last of the white slaves. By which he meant last of the colonials: a fixer, a smoother-over, a friend of British oil interests. When he met Christopher in Biarritz, he took him back to Saudi Arabia. Miles was so well liked that the diplomatic community protected his privacy and asked no questions.

What Christopher did in Saudi Arabia was another problem. After a bad argument, Christopher took a car that needed work and drove off to Jordan, where the princess liked him and would take him in. The car broke down in the desert, the only car on the road, and Christopher sat in the sand and cried, sure it didn't matter that he was wasting his body's water, because he was going to die. It was a hundred and ten degrees Fahrenheit, and he had no water with him. Finally a Bedouin bus full of sheep came by, and Christopher rode with the sheep all the way back to Riyadh, where he called Miles to come pick him up. "The smell in that bus, I was positively *reaching*," Christopher would say, telling the story.

(Miles had the precise and modulated accent of the British diplomat abroad, and he could keep a doomed luncheon alive, but there were words he'd made decisions about, and the decisions were wrong. "Retching" was one of them. He would say, "Well, it's a mute point." Of the Falklands War: "Those Argentine boys were platently not ready to fight." Christopher picked up each of Miles's mistakes without question.)

The desert rescue by the Bedouins was the last news I had heard from them. I knew they had split, and that Christopher wasn't forthcoming about why. But Miles had reclined on this dark terrace and told Eugénie everything—and now Eugénie was as forthcoming as she could be.

In the house in Saudi Arabia they employed two Arab servants, Eugénie said: a cook and a butler, both discreet and understanding about the sleeping arrangements. It was an embassy house, marble-floored against the heat, with a wing for the servants. The cook, a widow, kept to herself. An older man named Ahmed was butler and valet; he had worked for the old ambassador, and Miles considered him a friend. But Christopher disliked the old man, and finally threw a fit about the way the laundry was done. Ahmed resigned with grave dignity, and was replaced by a boy named Omar. Omar was handsome, lean and flirtatious in his movements, and Miles came home early one day to find him in bed with Christopher. Miles waited while Omar dressed and left the room. Christopher cried, and talked about how he missed his work in England (he had worked for an interior designer, choosing fabrics), and how bored he was, how he needed an outlet. Miles, unmoved by the tears, reflected that again Christopher was wasting water in a desert. He fired Omar, and a third man came to them. His name was Angelo and he was Filipino; he had come to the country with a diplomatic family. He was Catholic, and made time to pray. Miles was pleased to find him ugly—not deformed, but the proportions of his face and body seemed wrong. Christopher found Angelo ugly, too, and he frowned and clanked his knife and fork at meals.

"You're a physical snob," Miles told him.

"It's an aesthetic question," Christopher said. "It's about the beauty of your home."

Angelo had not been working for them long when things began to disappear. The idea depressed Miles as a sad cliché, and he ignored it until a houseguest had a pair of gold cuff links removed from his room. The cuff links were found in Angelo's things before he could fence them.

"Why were these in your room?" Miles asked him.

"I didn't steal them," Angelo said.

"Then how did they get there?" Miles asked.

The man shrugged, and didn't meet his eye.

Miles didn't want to fire Angelo; he liked him, and their position was delicate. Ahmed and Omar were already out in the streets resenting him, and he couldn't control what they did or said. "The next time it happens," Miles said, "I'm going to turn the matter over to the police."

The man looked up at him, alarmed, then looked at his feet and nodded. "So I can keep the job," he said.

"Yes."

"They cut off a hand."

"I know that," Miles said. The Hammurabic code had been softened to a three-strikes rule. In the case of theft, the first two convictions served as warnings, and on the third they did cut off your hand.

A few weeks later, Miles's watch disappeared from his dressing table, and he reported the crime, as he had said he would. While they waited for Angelo to come back from the police, or to call, Christopher smoked on the terrace, a rare nervous habit. A gaudy desert sunset hung in the sky beyond the city, and Christopher was breathtaking in the pink light: clear-eyed, with a wave in his hair. Miles had come closer to putting his heart in Christopher's hands, and being his completely, than he had with any other man. He could feel the reproach in Christopher's smoking.

"I can't believe you sent him in," Christopher said.

"You have to do what you say you will," Miles said.

"You know this country is barbaric. You sent him to those beastly police."

"They won't cut off his hand," Miles said. "It's a warning."

"It's a strike."

Miles put his arms around Christopher's shoulders and smelled the tobacco in his hair, the mint of his skin beneath.

"Why do I smoke these things?" Christopher said, putting out his cigarette. "I'll be a wrinkled old man."

The sky had grown dark, the pink light fading in blue. Christopher looked at him with sadness but without hatred, and Miles felt again that his heart might be safe.

For two days they went without Angelo, and without word from him. On the third morning, while Christopher was still asleep, Miles heard Angelo's voice in the kitchen. He tried to respect the kitchen as a private place for the servants, but he went in. The cook was making a strong-smelling tea. Angelo sat at the kitchen table and didn't look up.

"Third time for him," the cook said.

The bandage was white and clean, and wrapped Angelo's wrist tightly where the hand should have been.

"Why didn't you tell me?" Miles asked, and found he was genuinely angry. "I wouldn't have sent you if I'd known."

Angelo said nothing, but sat at the table and drank his tea. The cook looked at Miles with her hands on her hips until he left the kitchen.

At work that day, Miles was distracted and irritable. A case had fallen to him: an English girl had followed her lover home to Riyadh, discovered he was already engaged and murdered him in his sleep. The embassy had tried to get her extradited to England for months. The murder had been brutal, the young man from an important family, and no one was in a mood to let the English girl go home. Miles was tired of the whole affair, and it combined with Angelo's hand to make him guiltily stomachy. He went home early to find Christopher, red-eyed, packing brightly colored shirts in suitcases.

"I'm going home to England," Christopher said. "I've called already, I'm getting my job back."

Miles saw one of his own shirts go into a bag. "Why are you going?" he asked.

"Why do you think?"

Miles wondered why he had never tried to find Christopher

a job here, to keep him occupied. He could have helped the oil wives decorate their houses.

"You're cold," Christopher said. "You can maim a man and live with these monsters. I can't. I have to go home."

"Please," Miles said. It couldn't be said he hadn't suffered for the lost hand. That, anyway, was what Eugénie said.

"Don't *please* me." Christopher pushed past him to the bureau.

It came as a surprise to Miles that Christopher could go, but he did. He got on a plane without Miles's permission and went back to England, leaving Miles stunned and amazed. Christopher had been twenty-five when they met in Biarritz: an arrogant, pretty boy who liked to lie back, be adored, have things done to him, then order banana daiquiris from room service. Miles had gone along for a time, but Christopher had grown up since then, risen to Miles's challenges, become more interesting at dinner and in bed. The thought struck Miles that he had cultivated Christopher to the point where he could imagine living out his life with him, only to lose him to someone, to others, who wouldn't appreciate how far Christopher had come, and who might see the persistent boyishness as a reason for disdain, and not for love.

Angelo stayed on, a constant reproach. He fumbled at first, but soon became deft with the plates, holding a clean one tucked under his right elbow while he whisked another away with his good left hand. His skill was as excruciating to Miles as his fumbling, and Miles began to stay at the embassy late, so he could have his dinner left out for him and avoid being waited on by a man with such reason to hate him.

He had made no progress with the English girl's deportation. If she was found guilty, she could be executed in public. The executions were the thing that bothered Miles most about the country: he felt he acquiesced to them, since he had no power to object. The guilty were drugged, which was some consolation, dragged up to the platform, staggering, and pushed to their knees. The executioner jabbed them in the back with a sharp prod to make the spine arch and tighten the neck muscles, and then the sword came down. If the man was lucky, it came down straight. They tended to shoot women, to avoid exposing the neck and back, but the girl could be beheaded; it had happened. The British prime minister had halfheartedly asked for her return, and the queen had said nothing. The girl had no connections at home, no one fighting for her. Miles slogged on in her behalf, not to redeem himself for Angelo's hand, but because working late let him avoid Angelo altogether.

Three months into this new life, he received a letter and a package, delivered by a friend who had seen Christopher at a dinner party in London, and was on his way to Riyadh. The friend had brought the letter to Miles, and Miles had brought the letter to Eugénie. Someone was sent to look for it in her room. Eugénie feigned scruples about reading it to us, but in her excitement when the letter was found, she forgot them. It said:

Dear Miles,

I explained part of why I was leaving, but not all of it. Here's the thing. Angelo didn't steal your watch, or the cuff links. He didn't steal anything from us. He must have stolen things before, to get two strikes, but I didn't know about the strikes. I thought you'd just fire him the way you did Omar, I never thought you'd turn him in. But what I did wasn't any better.

I stopped liking me, and stopped liking you—that's what happened. I'm sending this with your friend (isn't it funny how everyone we know is "your friend"? We don't call anyone "our friends." It's always "Miles's friends." I keep noticing things like that lately. Someone corrected me saying "a mute point" yesterday and I realized I got it from you. Did you know it's wrong?).

So, no love to you except the old love, and that was real enough.

Christopher's signature was loopy, like an experimenting child's.

In the package, padded with tissue, wrapped in letter paper and sealed with mailing labels, was Miles's watch. The framing of Angelo made such sense and such little sense to him that he felt if he had been Christopher, he would cry.

He found Angelo in the narrow laundry room, ironing shirts, and said he knew Angelo hadn't taken the watch. He said the job was Angelo's as long as he wanted it, and he was deeply sorry for what had happened. Angelo set the iron upright with his good hand and straightened a collar, holding the shirt down with the severed wrist he kept pinned in his sleeve.

"God caught up with me," Angelo said. "I stole more than three times before I stopped."

Miles left the room, moved and disturbed. He couldn't go back to England, with the English girl needing him and Angelo needing the job. Saudi Arabia was his country now, and he felt at once mired in it and dispossessed. He was given an interview with the girl, after many requests, and they sat in a visiting room in the station where she was held. As soon as they were alone, she shoved off the black veil that covered her head and throat. The room was clean and cool, with pale blue walls, and she was unshowered but pretty: she had a heart-shaped little gamine's face.

"I'm trying to get you back to England," he said. "It would help if you presented yourself better." He didn't know how else to say this. There had been one television interview, and she had come off apathetic and cruel.

The girl laughed, and looked down at the dirty floor-length smock she wore. "How would I do that?" she asked. "Do you know what it's like in here?"

"Do they abuse you?"

"They know they can't," she said. "Because of you. So they just talk about it, but they talk about it all the time."

"Don't you want to go home to your family?"

She laughed again, a short, dry cough. "They'd lock me up for good there," she said. "They'd have to."

"Better than having your head chopped off."

The girl looked at him, blank-eyed, as if he'd switched to a language she didn't know.

"Isn't it?" he prompted.

"What?" she said. She was a Geordie girl and it came out "wot."

"Better," he said, but she had withdrawn into the silent trance for which she had become known by the Saudi authorities. It seemed to be triggered by threats. Miles wondered if he could get her declared unfit to stand trial, based on her trances, but the distinction wouldn't matter here.

Before he left the room, she stopped him. "My father worked in Kenya before," she said. "D'you know what the pidgin name for a solar eclipse is?"

"What?" He was disturbed by how much it sounded like "wot."

"'Hurricane lamp belong Jesus gone bugger-up,'" she said.

He shook his head with surprise. "Is that a joke?"

"It's real," she said. "I keep thinking about it. That's what my life feels like here."

Miles went home to the supper the cook had left for him. His meat was dry and the milk warm, with the first hint of spoiling. He threw the food away and began calling numbers of people in London who might know where Christopher was. After the sixth call, he got Christopher on the line. The voice sounded like youth and health, and made him furious. He wanted to say something about the watch, the hand, but couldn't risk Christopher hanging up.

"I miss you," he said. "It isn't good here."

After a long silence, Christopher said, "Well, come back to England, then."

It wasn't an invitation, and Miles heard his own reply as if he spoke from the bottom of a hole: "I have to stay for the girl."

"She's a killer," Christopher said. "Let the killers kill her."

"She's a sad girl."

"The world is full of sad girls," Christopher said. "You lucky sod—you're not responsible for a single one of them."

"I feel responsible for this one."

"Did you get my package? Is Angelo still working there?"

"Yes," Miles said. He spread his fingers flat on the marble counter, feeling the cool pressure of the stone. "Yes."

"How can you stand it?"

"I can't fire him," Miles said.

"Aren't you going to say anything about the watch? About what I did?"

"Oh, Christopher," Miles said. "What do you want me to say?"

Christopher hung up.

The string of appeals the Saudi court had been half humoring ran out, and the English girl was beheaded in private, as a diplomatic courtesy. The family declined to nominate an executioner, and Miles was allowed to pay the professional the extra, to be sure the blade was sharp and the blow clean. There was a brief flurry of news on the BBC and CNN, and the girl's body went back to her family in Newcastle, and then the story seemed to be over.

Miles went to bed. He told them at work he had a fever, and then he did have a fever, a bad one. He cried wretchedly, as he hadn't done since he was a child, over losing the English girl, her sun gone bugger-up. He cried over losing Christopher, and he cried over what Christopher had done, until his nose began to bleed and he stanched it with handfuls of tissues. When he stopped crying and bleeding, he flipped the pillow to the dry side and slept, and when he wasn't sleeping he listened to Angelo and the cook moving quietly outside his door.

On the third day Angelo knocked and brought in the tray Miles had been sending back with the cook, untouched. He balanced the tray on his severed wrist, and sat down on the edge of the bed to set it across Miles's lap. Miles studied the man through his feverish haze. Angelo's eyebrows were almost nonexistent. His nose was strangely small, and his upper lip withdrawn. His face was not evenly matched on both sides, but that was true of many people; the right eye was set higher, but both eyes were amber-colored and serious. His hair was cut short, and he was clean-shaven.

"You have to eat," Angelo said.

"I'm not hungry," Miles said.

"You die if you don't eat."

"I'm sick."

Angelo looked at him, and Miles didn't think he had ever been looked at so directly. The fever and the closeness of the man made Miles reckless.

"Why haven't you poisoned me?" he asked.

Angelo looked surprised. "You won't eat," he said. "How can I poison you?"

"I wish you would," Miles said, and he closed his eyes, embarrassed.

"They killed the English girl," Angelo said.

It was a diagnosis, not a statement of fact. Miles said nothing.

"If I can say it," Angelo said, "you should get out of bed." He left the room, closing the door with his good hand.

Miles looked at his food. Soft-boiled eggs, a bowl of soup, cold juice. He drank the juice and it cooled him. Angelo was right: it was time to get out of bed, to go back to his job, to smoothing over differences and making arrangements. There was nothing else he was good for. He was ravenous, and began to eat.

✦

"So, was he poisoned?" the Englishman asked. A boat with a red light raced by on the sea. The coffee cups were gone, and we sat with the empty table at our knees. The au pairs at the nearest house were having a party, and their voices carried through the dark, Danish and lilting.

"Of course not," Eugénie said. "He was here with me a week ago."

"And Angelo?"

"You sound like Christopher," Eugénie said. "Miles would never fire him."

A breeze came up, and Eugénie gathered her white wrap. The servants had long said good night, and all but the terrace doors were shuttered in case rain came before morning. The white cushions, except the ones we sat on, had been taken in.

"How can Miles stay there?" the young Frenchman asked.

"How can he leave?" I asked.

They all looked at me.

Eugénie stood. "Good night, my dears." Her shoes were like high-heeled doll sandals beneath her, and she tottered a few steps across the stone before finding her grace again. "*Bonsoir.* I'm going to bed." She waved over her shoulder with the corner of her wrap in her hand.

We watched her go, and sat in silence, alone with her house, watching the candle inside its glass shield flicker. My husband swung to his feet, levering his body out of the low, soft chair. "I'm going for the brandy," he said.

In the bay, the boats swung at anchor. There were no invading Turks, only the faint sound of laughing Danes. The English couple gazed at the lamp; the French boy studied his hands. The flame swayed, and I looked for something to fix on, but everything seemed swallowed up in the dark.

THIRTEEN & A HALF

ON THE MORNING of the eighth-grade dance in June, Gina woke to the sound of running water and the smell of papaya-mango-dewberry steam seeping under the door. She had an acute sense, listening to her daughter in the shower, that this was a fleeting moment in her life: the papaya-scented girl in blue eye shadow and body glitter would disappear as quickly as two and six and twelve had gone. Within a year, Amy would want to smell like perfume in tiny cut-glass vials, and Gina would never again wake to this tropical fog.

Her second-graders were already out for the summer, so the morning felt blissfully free. They exhausted her, but there was something comforting about the endless march of seven-year-olds. They never got any older; they wanted love more than independence; they would never be thirteen. Gina lay thinking of that unchanging procession of small bodies, then followed her daughter downstairs.

Her husband, Chase, had already walked down the road to get the paper, and now he sat in the living room reading a detective novel with environmentalist heroes. Amy stood at the kitchen counter, solemnly reading the funnies. Lanky and sandy-haired like her father, she wore soccer warm-ups that snapped down the side of each leg, a short-sleeved T-shirt with a flower on the chest, and rings with sparkling blue hearts and butterflies. Chase said thirteen-year-olds were like savages: you could buy Manhattan from them for a handful of beads.

Amy also wore a fiberglass walking cast that came up to the middle of her thigh. She had jumped from a tree and broken her ankle, and her metallic-blue toenails stuck out of the cast. Gina was torn: she was glad her daughter was still young enough to play in trees, but mystified at why she would jump out of one, a tall one. She had asked Amy why, and Amy said, "I felt like it." This secrecy was a new development.

"How's the cripple?" Gina asked.

"Fine," Amy said, abandoning the funnies. She poured a big bowl of Grape-Nuts and milk, and seemed to consider each bite while she ate. But she couldn't be thinking about Grape-Nuts, not the whole time.

"Who do you dance with at these things?" Gina asked.

Her daughter shrugged. "I guess it's like dances at camp. Some with boys, mostly with girls."

"There are dances at camp?"

Amy rolled her eyes.

"What are you going to wear?" It was a question Gina's mother would have asked; a question that would have driven Gina, at thirteen, to wear something shocking.

"This," Amy said, nodding at her soccer warm-ups. It could have been true.

"Is Dad going to pick you up after?"

"He's my dad, not yours," Amy said, but she poured her cereal milk into the sink and went to the living room to ask. Gina washed the white film down the drain and thought about getting Amy a fresh glass from the fridge—for the calcium, for her bones—but Amy would say drinking cold milk in the morning made her puke.

Amy returned from her father. "It's like talking to a wall," she said. She blew her bangs off her forehead. "Marisol's mom'll pick us up."

Gina walked her daughter outside, where the sun slanted yellow through the trees. "Dr. Fisher would skin me for letting you dance," she said. She wondered, briefly, if she could have gotten the doctor to forbid it. She didn't want Amy there untended.

Amy didn't answer, but threw her arms around the golden retriever in the drive, rubbing his sides and talking in his ear. "Yes you are, yes you are," she said. "Yes you are." The sun caught them, lighting up the hair of girl and dog like two flames. "Yes, yes, yes," Amy said. Then she carried her heavy backpack, with her odd, uneven gait, across the road.

Marisol, the best friend, lived in the only other house nearby. The access road to both houses was unpaved, to keep it passable in snow and ice. To the south, the road led to the mailboxes and the fairgrounds and town. To the north, it led to a beaver creek and tall willows. In good weather there was a hobo camp near the creek, where someone was once murdered with an ax. Gina held the dog's collar and watched Amy disappear through the brush. Beyond the hedges, she heard Marisol's mother tell the girls to buckle their seat belts. Three car doors slammed shut. Gina went inside to her husband.

"You could answer Amy when she talks to you," she said.

"What?" Chase placed his bookmark and looked at her over his glasses, his face blank and innocent.

"She asked you for a ride home."

"Home from what?"

Gina gave up, and went upstairs to see if there was any hot water left.

Their ten acres at the edge of town had been given to them by Chase's father, to build on. Gina had an image from that time of Chase on the roof with a hammer in one fist, and sawdust in his hair, and she had been deeply proud of him. He believed he could do things, like build a house, and so he could. But he had cut corners where he shouldn't have. The inside doors were flimsy, the ventilation bad, the hot water tank too small. And still Chase loved the house, and would never leave it.

He was gone when she came downstairs again. She did her end-of-school paperwork, then took the dog to the beaver creek, cutting wide around the empty hobo camp with its murdered ghosts. From the road she could see the whole valley, locked in by mountains. The dog raced ahead and doubled back to her, then raced ahead again. Inconsequential white clouds broke up the midday blue. This walk, with the flash of redwing blackbirds in the burdock, was the only thing Gina loved about the house. But Amy loved it with the automatic love of children, and it would be dangerous to take her away. She was too ready to dismiss her mother already. When Gina got back, there were men in the farthest field, wearing flak jackets, guns and radios. Two squad cars waited at the bend in the road.

At one o'clock that morning, in Helena, a hundred miles to the south, four boys had stolen a red Volare. The Murphy boys were brothers: Joe had jail time, Danny had a juvenile record for stealing tools from garages. Lyle Ribaud was off the Blackfoot reservation, and people said he would have been all right if he hadn't mixed up with the Murphys. Trey Jordan was only fourteen, a high scorer on standardized tests, a cleared suspect in his own father's death the year before. The gun the boys carried—a little Walther PPK—was Trey's.

The boys sat in the stolen Volare outside town drinking beer, talking about how nothing ever happened in Helena, how it was a boring, stupid town. Then they cruised past the drive-in, wishing it were open for burgers and shakes, and turned on Thirteenth. Joe Murphy drove slowly enough down the dark, sleeping street for Trey Jordan to fire one bullet through every front window for two blocks, each with a lovely, satisfying crash and shatter, until the two clips he had were empty. Then Joe headed north for Great Falls. It was 3:30 A.M., and they were gone before anyone knew what had happened.

By 5 A.M. the boys were out of gas in Great Falls. They pulled up at a minimart to fill the tank, but found themselves short of cash, and left with a friendly wave to the cashier. By five-fifteen they had crashed the Volare into a fairgrounds outbuilding with the cops behind them, and piled out to run. The police took Lyle and the Murphys into custody, but Trey Jordan and his gun were gone.

*

Gina didn't know anything about the boys when she saw the men combing the field outside her house. She locked the doors and called Chase at work, and he told her most of it. He had seen the wreck when he walked to get the newspaper at the end of the road, and he had talked to the police who were there.

"This was at six," Gina said.

"Five-thirty, six."

"And you didn't tell me about it."

"I didn't think much about it," Chase said. "You weren't up yet."

"I was up before you left. We talked."

"You were mad at me about something," he said.

"I sent Amy alone to get a ride. I went walking."

"Maybe I knew you'd react like this."

"Like what?"

"I'm on another call," he said. "We'll talk later."

Gina put the dog in the kennel and drove to Amy's school to wait outside until classes got out. Amy looked surprised and walked warily to the car, letting her leg cast slow her down more than it had to.

"I'm staying for the dance," Amy said. "They're just cleaning the gym."

"Where's Marisol?"

Amy shrugged. "Her mom said she'd pick us up."

"I don't want you to go anywhere but the dance."

"Why?"

"Just don't."

Amy cocked her head to one side. "First you're afraid of me going to the dance, now you're afraid of me not going."

"I never said I was afraid of you going."

"Yeah," Amy said.

Marisol came out of the school and gave Gina a languid, suspicious look from the other side of the street.

"I'm going to help decorate the gym now," Amy said carefully.

Gina watched the girls walk away into the building, on their long, too-long legs, Amy's cast not slowing her down at all. They leaned into each other to talk, and glanced back at the car. Amy made an impatient gesture with her hands. Gina drove to the library, to hide out while the police did their work.

At six, she drove home. The big field was empty. She stopped at the mailbox, thinking Chase would have been there already, but the mailbox was full. The dog whined behind the gate of the kennel, and Gina let him out. The front door was unlocked. She guessed Chase had come home and gone out again, without locking the door. That was crazy, under the circumstances, but if she told him so, he'd say she was paranoid. Standing in the entryway, she heard a man's angry voice upstairs. She couldn't make out the words, but a phone was put down, and then there was the sound of a cell phone ringing in the same room. Gina slipped out, caught the dog's collar and put him in the car, and drove to a pay phone to call the police. Three squad cars met her near the house five minutes later; one was the sheriff's.

"Stay in your car with the door locked," the sheriff said. The three officers drew their guns and disappeared on foot down the drive. Gina stayed with the puzzled dog, afraid the boy with the gun would appear, unsure what to do if he did. She had told the officers it was a man's voice upstairs, not a boy's, and she thought the sheriff must know something, to come with two men and act so alarmed. Gina had once owned a gun, a gift from her mother: a Saturday-night special with a mother-of-pearl handle. She had sold it when her mother died, but now she wished she had kept it in the glove box. She tried to reassure the dog, saying, "Yes you are, yes you are," but neither of them was fooled.

Ten minutes later the taller of the deputies appeared at the car window. She rolled the window down.

"Ma'am?" he said. "Do you have a husband?"

She nodded.

"We think he's upstairs watching TV."

Gina went in, and confirmed that the man in the living room in his T-shirt and boxer shorts was her husband. She avoided his eye. The T-shirt was an old white one, worn thin at the shoulders; the boxers were blue-striped.

"Don't you be embarrassed, now," the sheriff said. "You did the right thing. Never go into a house you think is dangerous. We'd rather get the call from you. Okay?"

Gina nodded.

"Okay, Chase?" the sheriff said, and his voice was friendly, conspiratorial.

"Sure," Chase said. He'd recovered himself, and didn't seem like a man in his underwear.

"There's been an armed fugitive out here," the tall deputy told Gina. "You did just the right thing."

The sheriff said, "We'll have him tonight. Don't you worry."

Gina waited until they were gone to close the door. The house was growing dim, and she turned on a floor lamp.

"What was that about?" Chase asked.

"I heard a man's voice."

"You know there's a TV up there."

"It didn't sound like a TV. It sounded like a man. I didn't see your car."

"My car's in the garage," he said.

She kept her distance. Chase would never hurt her, but neither would he forget being confronted in his boxers by three armed cops. She had once liked his anger and the intensity of his moods; it had seemed important that he felt things strongly. She closed the curtains on the field where the boy had run away. "I'm not going to live my whole life here," she said. "That's just not what I'm going to do."

It was a statement she had never made, never seriously, but she found she believed it, as much as she believed Chase would never come with her. Maybe not this year, maybe not till Amy was out of school, but she would go. She was grateful Amy was in town at the dance, not a witness to this scene. Amy might still believe that her parents presented a united front to the world, and Gina felt children should believe in the strength of that front.

"That man's out there," she said.

"A boy," Chase said. "He's just a boy."

At the dance, Amy and Marisol feigned casual conversation, eyeing the crowd in the darkened gym. They had danced, some in jumping circles with other girls, some slow with boys' arms around their waists. Marisol had been asked the most, being so glossily brunette and so tall. She had the legs and the sullen expression of girls in magazines, and the boys dared each other to ask her. She didn't always say yes, and it was hard to predict who would be refused. Her caprice was part of her appeal.

Amy knew she didn't have what Marisol had. She was freckled and pale, almost as tall as Marisol but ganglier. Her braces weren't off yet, and she had the walking cast. If she had known she would break her ankle jumping out of that tree, she might not have jumped, but at the time she had wanted to see the green grass coming up at her, fast. She wore a short skirt borrowed from Marisol, a skirt her mother would be afraid to forbid her to wear. But the boys didn't ask her to dance because of the skirt. They asked because she was a nice girl in a cast, and it made them good guys, and there was no harm in it. It was a funny joke to steer her, burdened with fiberglass plaster, in lopsided circles. She was a good sport, and was being one now. But she could feel their awe of Marisol, the heat of attraction coming off her friend.

Marisol leaned over to whisper to her, and when they looked across the room, a boy approached them. He wore jeans and a dark blue T-shirt, and the tear in the knee of the jeans looked like an accident. Up close the shirt might have had a mud smear across the shoulder, a brown smudge against the blue. The boy was looking at Marisol, and Amy knew the look, though the other boys tried to disguise it. Then he glanced at Amy and seemed to catch her understanding. He swerved toward her.

"You wanna dance?"

Amy couldn't speak at first, for surprise. The boy was good-looking, what Marisol called a Yummy. A little scruffy, but the best boys were. Amy tapped her cast below the bare thigh at the hem of her skirt. "I'm not too good right now."

"S'all right," the boy said. "I'm not too good either." A slow song was playing, and he took her in his arms, the way any boy would, with his hands around the small of her back. She turned easily on the rubber heel, accustomed to the movement by now, and she made a face at Marisol over his shoulder. Marisol raised her eyebrows.

He smelled like sweat, like the boys' soccer team when they scrimmaged together, but he didn't look like he played sports. She didn't mind the smell; it was only a sharp, boyish smell. He kept his head down, concentrating, like he didn't dance often. His hands were hot and damp at the small of her back: he was nervous, and Amy was moved. He had chosen her, not Marisol, and he seemed to have no friends at the dance to show off for, no need to prove he was a decent guy. She smiled at him when he looked up next, and he looked surprised. Then one of his hands slipped away from the small of her back. She didn't look down to see where it went, but her heart sped up.

"You're a good girl," he said. His face was close to hers.

"If you say so," Amy said, her voice light—it was something Marisol might say.

"I do," he said.

She smiled at him again. His hand came back to her hip, and slipped down over the back of her skirt. She caught her breath, though he barely touched the cloth.

"Shh," he said. His fingers brushed the back of her thigh. "You're a good girl," he said. "I mean it, you are."

She didn't think to look for Marisol—she couldn't think of

anything clearly—but Marisol wasn't there anyway; bored with this ordinary slow-dance, she had wandered away. Amy studied the boy's face, to see what he would do. Then something smooth and hard-edged that was not the boy's hand slipped into the back of her cast and pressed against her skin. The thing was warm, as warm as his hand, and pulled the cast tight against the front of her thigh.

"If you be quiet a little bit," the boy said, "it'll be all right."

"What will?"

"Everything," he said. His hand brushed the back of her skirt, and she managed not to gasp, and then it rested again at the small of her back. She tried to puzzle out the shape of the thing inside her cast.

"What is it?" she whispered. "I won't tell."

"Shh," he said. "Don't look. I'll find you."

Then he was gone, and Amy stood alone and watched him cross the gym floor, away from her. He stayed close to the folded-up bleachers, moving quick and careful, and then he disappeared among the boys who were just boys, who meant nothing to her, boys she saw every day of her life.

PAINT

MARIE WAS WASHING breakfast dishes at the sink, light from the east window gilding her hair and shoulders.

"Leave those," Jack said. He wanted the morning to last, wanted to linger over the coffee. He guarded his cup.

"It's almost done." She was dressed smartly for work, his tall and formidable wife, in pressed black trousers and a silver blouse. Her black hair, striped now with gray, was twisted up at the back. She studied an ice cream bowl Jack had left to dry the night before, then dropped it into the sudsy water.

"That was clean," he said.

"No, it wasn't." Into the water went the drinking glass he'd washed, the spoon.

"Marie," he said sharply. She looked at him in surprise.

"Just leave the damn dishes," he said. "Please. I'll do them right."

She finished in silence and dried her hands on a towel.

"I'll be late again," she said. "Don't wait for dinner."

She took her keys and was out the door. He heard the grinding noise of the garage door opening, then closing. The early gold through the window had diffused into ordinary daylight.

Jack washed his coffee cup carefully, dried it and put it away. An ache of uneasy regret settled into his chest: he had the whole day ahead of him to think about the pettiness of snapping about the dishes. Only two of his wells were viable now, pulling up just enough oil to stick him at home—not so little he'd given up on them, and not so much he could look for new leases. He wandered through the living room, pulling dead leaves off houseplants. He tried contemplating the storm windows he had put up the week before, what good protection they would be against the winter. But the ache remained, and he looked beyond the glass to the streaked planks of the back deck. The old stain had begun to wear away years ago, wind down from Canada and long months of snow working their way into the cracks of the wood. Marie had threatened to weatherproof it herself, but he always talked her down, intending to do it, and she'd finally given up. Now was the time.

Energized, he drove to the paint store in Havre to rent a water-pressure sander. He was surprised how big it was, but he was happy to have a real piece of machinery, not just a vague promise he'd made to Marie. The air was bright and chill, the first hard frost still weeks away. He felt invigorated, as he drove back home, by the prospect of a job he could see through to the end: an end that would be a good thing, not a dried-up well. Marie talked that way about the dishes. She worked as a shrink for the state; she said if you couldn't solve people's problems, you could still stand over a clean sink, a job completed.

The first chips of paint came off easy under the gun-shaped nozzle. He had to keep the nozzle moving, or the water dug into the wood and shot splinters at his ankles. So he swept the spray across the deck, watching the dark stain peel away.

When he finished, he took the sander back to the paint store and put the deposit toward all-weather stain. The girl at the counter was young and pretty, the age of his only son, and he found himself wishing Michael had stayed home. He imagined Michael marrying this girl, giving up the guitar and coming back from Portland, with his earring taken out for the wedding. (*How d'you expect to get a job with a hole in your head?* Jack had asked when his son came home with the silver hoop.) But Jack couldn't set Michael up in the prospecting business; there wasn't any business left to set up. And the girl was visibly pregnant beneath her orange paint-store jumper; he couldn't wish that on his son.

Jack told the girl he'd just sanded all the whitewash off the *H* the high school kids painted on rocks on the low hillside every year. He said he was going to paint the rocks brown so no one would have to see the damn thing anymore. The girl hid her braces with her hand to laugh, then smiled and dropped three wooden paint stirrers into his bag.

"Couple extra," she said. "Case you need 'em."

She *was* pretty, with glossy dark brown hair, and he thought about her on the drive home, thought about the high round breasts beneath the orange jumper, even thought about the braces. Would she think he was retired, shopping for paint in the middle of the day? He was old enough to retire but not rich enough yet; royalties still dribbled from his leases, and he always had his eye out for the next one, the strike-it-rich claim, the find that would take care of him for good. He'd tipped his cap to her at the door.

At home he made himself a sandwich on the clean kitchen counter and ate standing up, looking out the window. He had hoped for a while to con Michael into doing the deck—maybe offer him the beat-up blue pickup that wasn't worth selling. Michael wouldn't have to marry the paint-store girl (Jack wasn't sure now that he wanted to give her up); he could just come home and paint the deck and be around. They had three bedrooms, one for each of them: Jack, Michael, Marie, all in the house again. But Michael wouldn't come home. Jack found an old T-shirt and tore it into rags.

Out on the naked deck, he opened the first paint can with a screwdriver and bent to fish one of the stirrers out of the sack. He gave the paint a good stir and the smell made him blink. The wood seemed dry enough for a first coat before Marie came home. It was best to have things neat for her: explanations, surfaces, rooms. No crud on the bowl in the dish rack. He poured the deep auburn stain into a tray and began to roll it over the stubborn flecks of old stain, the streaks of gray weathered wood, the bright yellow grain the sander had exposed. The fumes made him light-headed and he hummed to keep his concentration.

When the paint in the tray ran out, he gave the can another stir and rested his weight on the wooden stirrer, which snapped in the can. His hand plunged into the thick wet stain, and the ragged point of the stirrer drove deep into his wrist with a sharp dragging feeling, snagging open veins along the way.

"Okay," he said. "Jesus fucking Christ."

Paint ran down his fist, and blood oozed around the edges of the wood embedded in his wrist. The loose piece in his hand was the size of a domino, and a good four inches of the stirrer stuck out of his wrist, so he guessed there were another four inches inside, up between ligament and bone. He wondered when his skin had gotten so fragile. He felt dizzy, and sat on the steps to clear his head, baring his teeth at the wound.

"Marie," he said. "Oh, damn."

He let go of his forearm and fumbled for the rags. Gritting his teeth, he wiped at his hand to keep the paint out of the bloody gash in his wrist. He thought of the girl at the paint store and wondered why she hadn't warned him of the dangers. He felt betrayed by her, stupidly furious at her, and he set the loose broken end on the paint-can lid to keep it off the deck.

His wrist was bleeding good now, and he tried to remember what to do in this situation. This was a situation. He couldn't remember if impaled objects should be removed or not. He was breathing hard, and wasn't sure he could stand up. The sun was low and he checked his watch to see when Marie would be home. A streak of paint hid the watch face, and he wiped his elbow carefully against the crystal, replacing the paint streak with blood. Seven o'clock.

"Come on, honey," he said. "Come on home."

He thought he must be in shock; he held his forearm tightly to slow down the bleeding and thought about getting to a phone. He leaned forward to try to stand, but his legs gave out beneath him, almost pitching him onto the lawn; he let his wrist go to catch himself and sat heavily back down.

Jack closed his eyes, thinking if he could calm himself, then he could get up from the steps and walk into the house and call someone, call Marie, maybe call an ambulance, though Christ knew what that would cost and he wasn't on Marie's insurance because of his heart. The darkness behind his eyelids seemed to expand and spin, and he opened his eyes wide. People drove themselves to hospitals with broken femurs and gouged eyes; he could damn well do it with a punctured wrist. He thought he could crawl to the garage, and he eased his body down, still clutching his arm. His elbow gave way, and he felt the sticky, damp stain of the deck against his face but couldn't lift his legs. His breathing grew heavier, inhalations sharp with the smell of new paint; he was breathing too hard, and he was cold, and when he closed his eyes the darkness came on again.

He wasn't sure how long he lay there, but when he opened his eyes the sky had gone blue-gray. He couldn't feel his legs at all. He'd been grinding his teeth the way he did at night sometimes, the nights of wells coming up dry and why-didn't-Michael-call and what-about-Marie. He felt a pulling in the back of his mind, an all-over tingling like anesthesia taking hold, and he struggled to stay alert. The sky was very dark and the stars were out in his peripheral vision. Finally he heard the automatic garage door grind open on the other side of the house, and after a minute a light went on in the kitchen, casting a warm yellow square inches from his head. Marie.

"Mmm," he said. "Marie. Maria."

Faintly, through the storm windows he had so proudly put up before Marie mentioned them, he heard the water running in the kitchen sink. Marie washing her hands. Marie washed her hands fifty times a day. She said the public health nurses all did it, and she damn sure wasn't going to stop just because Jack thought it was funny. His breathing had stepped up again, and there didn't seem to be much air left anymore. He rolled to get a better shot at the door with his voice.

"Maria," he said. He wouldn't tell her about the rubbery numbness of his lips, he would just show her the thing sticking out of his wrist. He wouldn't tell her about the tingling, twisted feeling in his good hand. The wound she could deal with, although it looked bad and his shirt was soaked with blood. The freezing-up of his body was too bad to tell, and he would have to keep it from her if he could.

He heard the clatter of metal against metal. His mustard knife thrown in the sink. He hadn't put the sandwich things away. But then she must know he'd been interrupted and left things unfinished. He took a great gasp of air to make room for the surge of hope in his chest. Another yellow square appeared on the deck, this time just behind his head. Marie in the hallway. The paint in his hair was dry now; he'd have to repaint the boards he'd messed up. But panic rose like bile from his stomach at the thought that he wouldn't repaint it, he would die here on the deck.

"Marie," he called, louder than before, as loudly as he could. The *r* sound was impossible to make with his lips frozen up. "Mah-wee!" He couldn't slow his breathing down.

It would serve her right, with all her worrying about his wildcatting, about the danger and the money. About the time he spent in the oil fields with drilling crews. About the house triple-mortgaged against the hope that the fluid mass below would come up oil, not muddy water. He would show her, dying on the back deck with two producing wells. Or would she show him? His brain was fogged and the question seemed hard.

"Mah-*wee*!"

It was colder now, he was sure, and he rolled himself around his wrist, protecting it. It was too gruesome to show her. Best to have an open wound she could bandage, not this thing protruding. He looked at his good hand in the dim light from the window, the fingers curling together against his will, and he forced them around the stirrer. He pressed his damaged wrist against his body to aid his grip, grimacing with rubber mouth at the pain. And then he pulled, whiting out the space behind his eyes in a bright momentary burst, until he held the bloody, splintered thing in his hand, triumphant.

"Hah!" he said.

His wrist began to bleed faster now, in warm, dark jets, the way oil came up from the ground in his dreams. He'd been right to leave the thing in, but was too tired to chastise himself. You were supposed to leave it in. His head was lower than his chest—was that good?—and he felt the blood pool below his Adam's apple and drip toward the newly sanded, newly painted, newly fouled-up deck. He wondered who would repaint it if she didn't find him now.

Marie was very quiet in the house. There had been no sound since the irritated clank of the mustard knife. She must be taking down her graying hair in the bathroom, smoothing Pond's cream on her tired face. He tried to remember how long it had been since they had shared a room at night. Ten years at least. When their son left she had taken his room, moving his books and his old guitar into the garage. She listed her reasons: Jack snored. He ate onions at night and smelled of them. He stole the covers; even when they used separate blankets, he stole hers. He woke her when he got up at five. She couldn't function without her sleep and God knew they needed her income, she said. Jack took to brushing his teeth more, and the separate blankets were his idea, but he didn't push the issue. Sleep didn't have to be sex, his son once told him when Jack found a yellow-haired girl in Michael's bed one morning, the two kids tangled in sheets. Sleep didn't have to be sex. As if they really had only been sleeping there, the girl bare-shouldered, her clothes and Michael's in a heap at the foot of the bed. Jack had joked about it with Marie. Then Marie, when she moved out of his bedroom, said sex didn't have to be sleep.

Jack lifted his legs and dropped them on the stair, hoping the thud would be louder than it was, unable to move his feet or hands, still trying to slow his breathing down.

He called his wife's name. She didn't have to rescue him; he just wanted her close. He regretted all their suspicions: hers not always unfounded, his not easily dismissed. All the time she spent at work, all the nights she came home late. The cops called her out in the middle of the night to interview criminals, and he had wondered about those men: some of them Cree like her grandmother, off the Rocky Boy reservation, some of them violent white boys with no place to go. He wondered what they made of her, coming to them in their dark hours. The sheriff and his young deputy watched through an open door because Havre had no two-way mirror, and Jack wondered about them, too, watching his handsome wife, her long fingers folded in front of her, her black hair tied back, the serious look on her face when she listened.

"Your wife is something else," the sheriff had said to him, lighting up a cigarette outside the state liquor store, watched by his own quiet wife.

In the house, the water in the kitchen came on again. Marie washing her milk glass (no intention of losing her good strong bones), washing Jack's sandwich plate. Marie's hands in the warm soapy water, running the pads of her fingers around the lip of the glass, along the length of the knife. Shaking the drops from her hands before toweling dry. The kitchen light went off, the hall light stayed on. Jack thudded his feet on the stair again, more faintly; he couldn't lift his legs more than a few inches. "Mah-wee," he called again.

He wondered if the girl at the paint store would feel bad. If she would cry when she heard the news, her hand hiding her braces in horror, and tell her friends it was "too weird." He wondered if Michael would come home, for his mother.

The last light went out and the dark closed in on the deck again. Marie was going to bed. She must think he was in his room, asleep. She must be taking care not to wake him, walking through the house in socked feet, closing doors with a hand on the knob, without a sound. He held his wrist against his chest but no longer felt anything in it, nothing to distinguish the drained limb from the tingling ache in his whole body, radiating out from the core. They would find him in the morning and guess at what had happened. Marie spoke to failed suicides— Jesus, what would she think? She would be in her bedroom now, slipping off her socks, dressed in an old T-shirt worn silken with age. He called her name again, his voice hoarse and strange to his own ears. If there had ever been a time when he needed her to listen, needed her to hear . . .

He let his wrist fall away from his chest—no need to hold it if it didn't hurt—and let his head roll back to look at the sky. Brightest stars in the whole world, up on the hi-line. Nothing between here and there: no light, no cloud. The darkness filling his head now, the steady pull—no, not pull, not consciousness draining away but numbness creeping in, taking over the space inside his skull. And Marie sliding bare legs between cool sheets, stretched out the length of the bed, all her own, and falling into sleep, to wake with the cold morning sun.

THE
ICE HARVESTER

AN ICE HARVESTER appeared at the edge of the lake, pushing his ice cart. Each of the houses on the lake had a Frigidaire or an Amana Frost-Free; one had a professional Viking with brushed stainless-steel doors in which the children could see the blurred outlines of themselves when they went for the milk. No one needed to buy ice to keep the milk cold. The ice harvester was obsolete.

There was still a number for him, in the codes in the files in the workers' compensation building, files from before it was work*men*'s compensation, from when it was still the Industrial Accidents Board. Code 871: Ice Harvester. There were figures, under Code 871, determined by actuaries, to represent the inherent danger of the work. Harvesters were lost every year, when there were harvesters. The ice harvester who appeared when there was no need for him didn't know he had a number, but it would not have surprised him.

He stood at the edge of the lake and looked out at the ice. It had frozen over in a cold snap, and then a day of warm sunshine melted the surface, before the temperature dropped again, leaving the ice smooth as a mirror. The sky was overcast now, so the ice was white. He stood with his tools—a wheelbarrow, an ice saw, tongs, gloves—and considered the best place to start. The lake was curved like an organ of the body; in one of the indentations was a spring. The ice harvester picked up his wheelbarrow and started across the ice toward the spring. It was best to start where the water helped, where the ice was new and clean and wanted to be broken up. But springs were unpredictable; that was why harvesters were lost.

He walked on the ice in the flat-footed way of one who knows not to hurry, or glide, or carry his weight too far forward and let his feet slip out from under him. He made the most of friction. His boots were warm, as they had to be, with heavy leather soles, but he felt the cold making its way through the leather and the wool lining. It wasn't cold enough to cause discomfort, but it made him feel the ice was real. When he neared the spring, he was careful, keeping track of the delicate white cracks that shot down through the ice: still a good fifteen inches before the dark water flowed below. He saw a fish, silver and motionless, trapped in the ice, midswim. He listened for sounds of breakup, and slowed his walk.

There were rushes and cattails near the bank, and most were frozen in place, except where the spring came up; at the spring, the cattails emerged from black water, and the water cut into the frozen mass. The harvester stood near the place where the water began, and took his saw from the wheelbarrow.

The muscles in his back were strong, although he was old. He slipped his saw into one of the cracks caused by expansion, and worked it through the ice until the blade became hot with the motion. The triangular block he finally cut had two smooth edges from the hot steel. With the tongs he dragged the block from the water, then lifted it with his gloves. As he worked, he stacked each block in the wheelbarrow like stones in a wall, the lopsidedness of one making room for the angle of another.

He worked steadily, but the wheelbarrow was only half full when the sun rose to late morning, dull yellow behind the gray sky, and people began to come out of the houses. They pulled on hockey skates and figure skates, sitting on the bank while they struggled with tongues and laces. The children shouted to each other; the smallest ones skated behind small wooden chairs to keep their balance; some of the mothers brought hot chocolate made with milk kept fresh in the Frigidaire. The ice harvester worked on. He liked the sounds of the skaters, and he was careful not to break good skating ice. He was working and they were not, but they had their work at other times, and he was happy to have his. It was good to have them there.

A girl skated close to him, wearing a single braid and a winter hat. She was about seven, careful and well taught, watching the cracks in the ice to be sure of the depth. She studied the stacked wheelbarrow and waited, as if people usually explained things to her before she had to ask.

The ice harvester straightened his back and felt his tired

muscles arrange themselves in their upright places. "Good morning," he said.

"It's almost lunchtime."

He looked at the sky. She was right.

"Does your family have a refrigerator?" he asked.

"Yes."

He leaned on his saw, stretching first one shoulder, then the other. "Do you know anyone without one?"

She thought about it. "No."

"No," he said. He turned back to his work.

"What will you do with the ice?" she asked.

"Put it in my cart."

She looked across the lake to his tin cart waiting for him on the bank where he had appeared that morning. It was the cart he had pushed through town to sell the ice, when there had been people to buy it.

"When will the lake melt?" she asked.

He looked at the sky again and thought about the shape of the year. "Maybe March," he said. "Maybe later."

She calculated. "We can't swim till June."

The harvester waited for the child to leave, so he could continue with his work. He didn't know about swimming, and didn't know what to tell her. His expertise was restricted to frozen water.

"Are you warm enough?" she asked him. It was a question she was used to hearing; there was mimicry in her voice.

"If I keep working, I'm warm."

She nodded. It was that way with skating. She did a little figure eight, the only trick she had learned yet to do, and skated away.

As she left, there was a sound like a gunshot, and some of the skaters cried out, then laughed. The ice deep in the lake was shifting in the sun. The ice harvester listened, trying to tell, from the memory of the sound, where the shifting was. Across the ice, the little girl took her father's hands and skated backward. The noises weren't dangerous as long as the air stayed cold; the skaters were right to be unconcerned. He began to work again, cutting and stacking the ice. He had lost time talking to the girl. But she had made him think about swimming, about how the ice he worked so hard to break would melt away in summer until people could move through it instead of over it. He had never learned to swim; if a harvester fell in, it was not his ability to swim that was called on. It was his ability to kick and climb his way out in his heavy clothes, and to keep himself warm. The ice harvester knew he could kick his way out, if needed. He was not a man who would drown.

He worked until the wheelbarrow held what it could, stacked as efficiently as he knew how. He couldn't let it sit in the sun too long, or the blocks would melt and fuse together. There was one last piece, a good-sized block with smooth edges all around, as smooth as the surface of the lake, and he worked it out with the tongs until his foot slipped, the dark water swallowing his boot and his leg to the knee.

He dropped his weight to the ice then, leaning away from the hole; he inched backward, recovering his leg. He hooked his tongs around one leg of the heavy wheelbarrow, to hold on if the ice broke again. Only then did he feel the dull pain in his ankle from the freezing water in his pant leg and his boot. He was done now, for the day. He left the good, smooth-sided block where it floated, and lifted the handles of the wheelbarrow. The load was heavy, and the single wheel weaved drunk-enly ahead of him if he didn't hold the handles tight.

The wet boot was a discomfort, but not the worst thing that could have happened. The loss of the great, smooth block could be sustained. The unsteady wheelbarrow kissed the bank where he had left the tin cart. In the cart was a bag of the saw-dust they had given him at the old mill, when the mill was there, and he packed it around the blocks in the cart to keep the ice from melting. A light snow fell, settling on his shoul-ders and the surface of the pond. The cart called for a different skill in stacking, as it was narrower than the wheelbarrow and had deeper walls and a lip at the top, but the arrangement of the blocks held the same absorption for him, in the fitting together. It was work, but it made him feel at ease.

The cart took two loads, but he couldn't do another today, not with a wet foot. He hid the empty wheelbarrow in the bushes and picked up the handle-end of the cart. It was lighter than usual, but still heavy, and well stacked. He rolled it up the bank, toward the place where the old dirt road had been twenty years ago, before they blasted the tunnel in the hillside and paved a shorter road from town. He left, with each pair of steps, one wet leather-soled footprint that cut through the light snow to the ground, and one dry that tamped down a white outline of itself.

The family with the Viking refrigerator with the brushed-steel doors finished skating, and studied the footprints the man had left behind: one dark, one light. The prints, separated by a narrow wheel track, continued into the trees and saplings that grew in the abandoned roadbed. The children asked why—why the different footprints, why the old road, where it went. Their father, who usually had an explanation for everything, had none at all. He lifted his smallest boy to his shoulders in place of an answer, taking the boy's skates and his hockey stick in his hands. Other skaters followed them and went home to lunch, to warm, lighted kitchens and all the things they kept cold.

A STAKES HORSE

IT WAS EIGHTY-SOMETHING and dust-dry the first weekend of the state fair in Great Falls, and my father and I were at the races, as usual. We'd spent half the summer weekends of my life at dusty tracks, in dusty towns. I came from checking on the horses to find my father under a shade tarp at a picnic table, a straw hat covering his bald head. He looked tired.

"Take your drugs?" I asked.

He glared at me over his wire-rimmed dark glasses, and put a freckled hand down flat on the table. "Addy," he said.

I tried not to look at his hand on the scarred blue wood. Since he'd been sick I kept a sterile kitchen and carried antibacterial spray in my pocket, but then he'd sit at grimy, gum-spotted tables, and cross the track as the wind blew dried manure in swirling gusts. I couldn't spray everything, so I'd stopped fighting him about it. There had to be some trade-off for him, some reason for putting up with the painkillers and germ-killers and bone marrow–killers.

"Do you think the jockeys throw races?" I asked him.

There was a silence while he studied the odds board across the track. "I think a guy works awful hard to be throwing races," he said.

"But if it earns them a chance to win," I said. "If they take turns."

He shook his head. "I guess it happens."

"Would Connell do it?"

"I don't think so," he said.

My ex-husband had just ridden our fastest horse, a filly we called Rocky, to a surprising loss. My annulled husband— we weren't married long enough to earn the "ex." One of twelve kids from a two-room shack in Tennessee, Connell was the best kind of jockey: an athlete, addicted to nothing but racing, gentle with the horses and liked by the crowd. He was my height, too tall to make it in the South as anything but an exercise rider, so he came north, and when I met him he was the star of the Montana circuit. People would bet on anything he rode. That November I got myself up as a bride, but before the winter was over my new husband left for New Mexico. He couldn't stand the cold, he said. I wasn't invited. My father was sick by then, so I moved back into his house and swore off jockeys for good.

In the beginning I was just picking up slack, registering the horses for races when my father was in the hospital or when the treatments had tired him out, but it started to take most of my time just to keep us solvent. Even in remission he was tired, and the money wouldn't be there when he needed full-time care. He said he would rather have the horses than full-time care, and I could never argue.

When Connell returned to Montana, my father put him up on our horses again. At first I thought he was getting back at me for marrying Connell in the first place, but then I decided he was being loyal to a man who had done him no wrong and who was good at what he did; we needed purses to stay in business and Connell brought the horses home.

So when Connell lost what should have been a hand ride, and a purse that had our money in it in entry fees, I lost patience with him. I'd guessed before at what went on in the jockeys' trailers, when it was someone's birthday or someone was owed a favor or wanted revenge. When I'd asked Connell, he said what my dad said: "A guy works awful hard keeping his weight down to be throwing races." But there's such a feeling of impotence when a horse comes out of the gate representing everything you've worked for, and there's nothing more you can do. I wanted to keep what wasn't left to chance where I could see it.

"I think I want someone else up for a while," I told my father at the picnic table.

"I don't want anyone else up," he said. "I like Connell, and Rocky likes him."

I thought he must have felt, as I did, that Connell had let us down; I figured he was defending him in order to oppose me. The more my father weakened physically, the more he sought out conflict. Problems with the horses—losses, illnesses—put him in a stubborn mood. I let it go, and we watched the rest of the races in silence. My father's reticence had always felt to me, with country-song logic, like eloquence and generosity; we knew each other so well we scarcely needed to talk. But I'd begun to feel the pressure of limited time. I wanted to know what he knew, but I didn't know what else to ask.

It rained all week, and my father caught a summer cold and stayed home the second weekend of the fair. He thought he might come later in a separate car, but I didn't want him to drive the eighty miles to Great Falls alone. The track was sopping wet; they had run the sealer over the mud, to jiggle the water to the surface to evaporate, but it hadn't dried yet. I surveyed the crowd: maybe a hundred people standing around the paddock and the betting windows, maybe not that many. The huge old firetrap grandstands nearly empty at the biggest race meet of the year. It was true, what they said: racing was dying. People put their gambling money in poker machines.

I wanted to make sure someone had put mud shoes on Rocky; she had done all right in the mud before, and two more wins would make the summer worthwhile. When I got to the backside stables, Connell was there. He'd just finished taping Rocky's rear hocks.

"I hear you're mad at me," he said. Rocky turned her ears to listen to his voice.

"Not mad, exactly," I said. "You didn't have to tape her."

"I had some time and couldn't find your trainer. She gets cut up easy."

Rocky meditatively kicked one wrapped rear leg out behind her, shifted her weight and kicked the other. She looked sleek and calm. We'd bought her mother from our trainer as a favor; the trainer was disgusted with the mare, but my father liked the look of her, and she paid off in Rocky, a straight-legged filly who'd climb into your lap if you let her. The mare died at Christmas a year later, and my father didn't speak for days.

I put an arm around Rocky's neck and she nibbled at my tank top.

"I thought she should have won last week," I said. "The other horses are hit-or-miss but I count on her to win."

"They knocked her into the rail," Connell said. "She'll win today."

"Well," I said. "It's a tougher field."

"You want her to win?" he asked, and he gave me a hard look. He hardly ever made eye contact with me since he'd come back. He was usually looking at a horse or off into the middle distance, expecting weather.

"Of course," I said.

"Then she's going to win."

I felt embarrassed, more than I'd felt at his hearing I was angry, more like I used to feel when my father knew I was hanging around the paddock at the end of the day, waiting for a jockey.

Connell shook an aerosol can of PAM cooking spray, brushed off one of Rocky's front hooves and sprayed inside the shoe, to keep the mud off. The announcer called the loading of the eighth. We rinsed Rocky's mouth with a garden hose because we couldn't find the syringe, and the trainer's wife showed up on a stocky gray mare to lead her across the track. In the paddock, a jockey from the seventh race hosed off his white pants while another in splattered silks waited.

Rocky was on the outside again, so she would load last and wouldn't have to sit in the gate with wraps on her ankles.

Everything seemed good. Connell was supposed to save her in the first third of the race, then let her go. The old helpless feeling came on as I watched him get ponied onto the track and toward the gate. Nothing to do but wait.

And Connell didn't save her. She took the lead out of the gate and held it around the turn, running faster than I'd ever seen her run. When they came past the stands, she was two lengths ahead. "They never come home," the man next to me said as the horses ran down the backstretch. "The ones who break early never come home." But Rocky was six lengths ahead on the final turn, and ten lengths ahead past the stands and the finish—an easy win. A woman in front of me hugged her husband, and the man beside me dropped to his seat, disgusted. Usually the helpless feeling dissolves into euphoric relief when they win, but I didn't feel giddy or even pleased. I felt like there was something I hadn't been told, or something I hadn't understood.

Connell caught my eye in the winner's circle while Rocky stamped and sweated beneath him. I used to love to see him in the winner's circle and know he was mine, my love, my prize. Now I was stunned, for a minute, that we'd taken him back as a jockey.

"You didn't hold her in," I said, shading my eyes to look up.

"I was holding her," Connell said. "She's the fastest horse out there."

The shutter clicked for the win picture, and he swung Rocky in a tight circle back toward the stables on the other side of the track.

*

I waited for Connell by the paddock. I didn't want to. I'd put in my time waiting by the paddock. He grinned at me when he showed up, in a baseball cap and a racetrack jacket.

"Did she really win because she was the fastest?" I asked him.

"The fastest doesn't always win," he said. "But yeah, she's the fastest."

"Did you know she'd win when you told me she would?"

He studied me for a minute. "You know what, Addy?" he said. "This is a business. The track has to make money to stay open. The state has to make money just like they do off the lottery. Me and the other jockeys, we have to make money to eat. Those horses are running so the old boys in the stands can waste a Sunday and the rest of us can live our lives. That's all."

It was the longest speech I'd ever heard him make, and I still wasn't sure I had an answer. I said, "I didn't understand what was happening when we talked earlier—"

"Nothing happened."

"So I don't know if I agreed to anything. I don't want to know if I would have agreed. But they're my dad's horses and he wouldn't, ever, so it can't happen that way again."

"You need the money as much as anyone," Connell said. He pushed the cuffs of his jacket back to his elbows with two quick shoves, like we were going to fight, then tugged the cuffs down again. I watched his hands. I had loved his hands when I met him; they were deft and strong and sure.

"It has to be fair," I said.

Connell shook his head a little. "Anything can happen out there," he said. "Jesus. I thought you'd know that by now."

"As fair as it can be."

Connell shook his head again, tight-mouthed, and looked out at the track.

I drove home alone and tried not to think about what had happened or what might happen again. Instead I made plans to feed the half-wild barn cats, and water the plants, and call the doctors for the bottom line about my dad's driving.

My father already knew about the win when I got there. I'd forgotten we had a reason to celebrate. He was at the door, smiling his old invincible, take-on-all-comers smile. He looked almost healthy, and happy, the way he was back in the flush years. "You win some, you win some," he'd told me then. I sat next to him on the back deck and he clapped a freckled hand onto my knee.

"Wish I'd been there," he said.

Out in the pasture one of the new fillies, a strawberry roan, caught up to its mother to nurse as she grazed.

"Connell says it's all about money," I said. "He says it's just a business. Getting and spending."

"He's got it backward," my father said. "The money stuff goes on so we can all watch them run."

The yellow aspen quaked along the fence. The deck needed repainting and I picked at the flecks on the weathered wood. I tried to think of something that seemed important enough to say but not too sad to talk about, and could think of nothing.

The third weekend of the meet started well. My father's white blood cell count was up, and he drove, in defiance of the doctors. He seemed not to fill up the driver's seat the way he used to when he drove everywhere, a hundred miles an hour, and never got pulled over. We left early, heading into a pale sunrise, and somewhere on the winding road through the canyons it turned into a hot, dry day. I sat with my feet up on the dash, lead ropes and old race programs on the floor beneath me, and watched the mountains and the impossibly blue sky go by. I'd seen this landscape so much that most of the time my senses were glutted and one mountain range looked like the next. At other times, and this was one of those, it caught me by surprise and the blue was so vast and bright I couldn't breathe.

We parked near the empty stands. Dew still clung to the tough desert grass around the fences, and the state racing steward was working on his first beer of the day. "Fella from Wyoming," I heard him say.

Rocky was running a stakes race with the biggest purse of the summer and she was the favorite, even against a black filly named Provincial Lady, who'd beaten her in Spokane. She looked good: healthy and watchful. She never sweated before a race, never got uptight. Her stall was dark, with the musky chemical smell of clean horses and their medicines, and she knocked her head against my hands. I slipped under the rope to stand near her, and she shivered in one rippling motion from her neck to her haunches, and swished her tail. She lifted one foot to step away from me, then stayed. I felt a sudden, aching rush of love for her, a tightness in my lungs. I ran my hand along her nose, told her she had wings.

"Here to watch your filly win?" a voice behind me said, and there was Connell, wearing an unfastened padded vest, come from exercising horses at dawn.

"Look at her," he said. "That's a horse who knows how fast she is."

"She always looks like that," I said.

"That's true," he said.

Beneath my arm on Rocky's neck I felt her breathing. Her ears were turned toward Connell. "I don't want her to win if she can't win fairly," I said.

Connell did his trick of gazing off to the horizon and he frowned, then turned on me a brilliant smile. "I feel good today," he said. "I don't think I can lose."

The announcer read the lineup for the first race.

"See you in the winner's circle," Connell said, and he walked off toward the track.

The only last-minute way out of a race without a vet is if the horse goes over in a fit and hits the ground, and even then the paddock judge can claim not to see it. Rocky was calm and healthy; I couldn't get her to throw a fit at the gate. The horses came back from exercises, drenched and snorting, heads checked, and I tried to think what to do.

The boy in the race office gave me a wary look. He was skinny, and wore a fat braided belt with a trophy buckle. "You're pulling your horse? Is she sick?"

"No, I just want to pull her."

"Programs are printed; you need a vet," the boy said.

I studied his annotated program and decided to try lying. "I don't think she's in shape for seven furlongs," I said. "What about the eighth?" He had a ballpoint mark across the eighth race, a claiming race; one of the four horses in it had scratched.

"Five furlongs," he said. "But someone scratched so it won't go off."

There are claiming races at every meet, with a set claiming price; they're designed to even the field, to keep overqualified horses out. Any horse entered can be bought, before the race goes off, for the set price. But it doesn't usually happen, especially at the end of the season, when nobody wants more horses to feed.

"Anyone claiming today?" I asked the boy. He had a padlocked toolbox in the corner, with a slot in the top where you dropped your money if you wanted to buy. The one time we'd claimed a horse, we couldn't write a check before post time; we'd drained our checking with hospital bills and had to take the money out of our horseman's account, the one that paid the jockeys.

"Not with racing so bad," he said.

"I'll be back," I said. "And I'll need a jockey. Maybe the girl." I was embarrassed not to remember her name.

The state race steward was still standing by the beer window. He put his arm around my shoulders and hugged me sideways to show me to the tall cowboy he was talking to. "I've known this gal since she was two," the steward said. "Running around here with an ice cream bar all over her, just like she owned the place."

It was going to be easier than I thought; I edged him away from the cowboy.

"I dunno, Addy, it's a claiming race," he said. "You don't wanna put a stakes horse in a claiming race."

"The race won't fill otherwise," I said. "There's time to tell the handicappers."

"Does your dad know you're doing this?"

"He just wants to watch that horse run," I said. "This is the last chance until next year." I didn't say anything about the possibility of not having a next year. I'd lie and call in favors but I wasn't ready to play that card.

"You'll forfeit your stakes money," the steward said.

"That's okay. Better than hurting my horse in a long race."

He looked hard at me. "You mad at your dad about something, Addy?"

I blinked stupidly for a second. I was—I was mad at him for getting sick. For having faith in jockeys. For being corruptible in body and incorruptible in mind.

"God, no," I said.

The steward sighed and drained his plastic cup. "All right," he said. "Let's do it."

I asked the boy in the race office to hold the announcement until I found my father, but Connell had already heard, and he stopped me on my way out.

"That's a claiming race," he said.

"No one will claim her."

"I would have ridden her," Connell said. "Does your dad know about this?"

My father came from the dark under the stands, and I told him I'd put Rocky in the eighth, with the girl up. He reached for the program in his back pocket.

"I think she's crazy," Connell said.

My father left the program where it was. "The eighth," he said. "Then we've got time to kill."

Connell turned on a heel and stalked off toward the paddock.

It was like any other day at the races from there, spent checking on the horses and talking to people who'd known me since I was two. People asked about the switch and I talked about the length of the race and Rocky's lungs. My dad didn't ask me anything at all. By afternoon, summer thunderheads had moved in from the Smith River valley over the far side of the track. My father and I found a seat in the open stands.

"Why'd you take her out?" he asked finally.

"The race was fixed," I said.

"That's no reason to quit."

"It was fixed for us," I said. "So I didn't see it as quitting."

He fell silent again. The stands were almost crowded; people had come out. A man teaching his waist-high son how to bet told him this was a good race for picking a trifecta because there were only four horses to choose from. At three minutes to post, Rocky was at even money, and the man explained to his boy that even money wasn't worth your wager. At two minutes to post the announcer said Rocky had been claimed by someone whose name I didn't recognize, for the set price.

My father looked at me. "Claimed," he said.

I unrolled my program to look for the owner whose name had been announced. He was from Wyoming, with a Kentucky-bred filly in the ninth. "I didn't think anyone was buying," I said.

My father nodded.

"End of the summer," I said.

It started to rain, settling the dust and packing it down one drop at a time, but I couldn't bring myself to move. My father was wearing a warm jacket. When my face was good and wet with rain, I let the tears come. We watched the odds toss Rocky in and out of the favorite position until post time, when she loaded quietly into the gate on the other side of the track. The four-horse spun and shied, and then they were off. They came by the stands in a tight pack with Rocky moving in on the rail. The little boy's father shouted for the three.

I stood as they rounded the backstretch with Rocky in the lead, and everyone was roaring. The far side of the track looked hazy in the rain. Rocky lugged into the rail, slowing, and the pack began to gain. The three-horse, running wide, found a last-minute kick and passed the whole field on the final stretch. Rocky barely held on to third. The betting father hugged his son and pushed him out of the stands to collect at the window.

I sat down on the wet bleachers, and my father dropped his hand on my knee. "What're you crying for?" he asked.

"We lost Rocky," I said. "I lost Rocky."

He squeezed my shoulders. "All right," he said. "All right." He pulled away so I'd look at him. "I'll still get to watch her run."

The rain was coming down hard, and the stands where we sat were empty. I was wet and my nose was running, but I didn't want to move.

"If you don't chase me out of the rain," he said, "I'll have to do it myself."

I choked back a laugh. "Get out of the rain."

"That's better," he said, and we dragged ourselves out of the stands.

We stayed for the stakes race Rocky would have been in. Betting was light. Provincial Lady stumbled in second place, throwing the jockey into the infield, and had to be taken off the track in a van.

My dad went to the backside to see Rocky, and I signed papers in the race office, giving her over to the new owners. Then I stood alone under the dripping shade tarp, among the blue picnic tables, holding a folded check drawn on a Wyoming bank. The race steward came by, but he didn't meet my eye and I didn't want to talk to him.

Bettors headed out through the mud, dropping losing tickets on the ground. Two little girls in jeans and matching turquoise rodeo shirts hurried to the parking lot with rocking, cowboy-boot gaits. Connell, in his racetrack jacket, ducked under the shade tarp with me.

"The best-laid plans," he said.

His hair was wet from the shower, and he smelled like soap. Behind him I could see my father coming from the paddock, carrying Rocky's win blanket from the week before.

"You can ride her for the new owners," I told Connell.

Connell frowned, then shrugged. "I guess I can," he said.

We said good-bye at the gate, and my father took my hand and squeezed it tight. "You take it all too personally," he said. I followed him to the parking lot, through the muddy rain.

In the morning my father was picking up rocks in our field because the pastured horses were getting stone bruises. I tried to convince him to go back inside. He said he would after I helped him clean up the hay by the feeder.

"If I'm going to get sicker, it'll be from people," he said. "Horses are clean."

The horses had picked out the alfalfa from a new batch of hay and left piles of oat straw on the ground. My father decided that rather than let the leftovers rot in a pile, we should spread them around the field to mulch. He hoped some of it would seed, and I didn't argue. I raked trampled straw into piles, and he lifted it to the truckbed in forkfuls of shiny gold.

When we had filled the truck, he climbed in with his pitchfork to scatter the hay. I rolled down the window, sitting on the edge of the seat to get the clutch in, and started the engine. The radio blared on and I fumbled for the volume.

In the rearview mirror my father leaned on the pitchfork for balance. I let the clutch out in the compound gear and the truck rolled itself forward. He rocked and recovered in the mirror, and pitched the hay out in dusty yellow clouds. His face was red under his hat. At the far corner of the field I braked, and his breathing grew easier until he gave me a thumbs-up in the mirror to start again.

He held on while I turned the truck around, and we headed back across the dry late-summer field. The wind changed direction and blew a storm of golden straw through the open window into the hot cab of the truck. I rolled the window up against the flurry, and the flakes spun in the light as we drove back to the barn for another run.

ABOUT THE AUTHOR

Maile Meloy was born in Helena, Montana. She received the Aga Khan Prize for Fiction for the best story of 2001 in *The Paris Review*. Her stories have also appeared in *The New Yorker* and in *Ploughshares*. She lives in California.